The Sand Eggs

The Sand Eggs

To

Monica

Best wishes

[signature]

Hookline Books

Published by Hookline Books 2013
Bookline & Thinker Ltd
#231, 405 King's Road
London SW10 0BB
Tel: 0845 116 1476
www.hooklinebooks.com

A CIP catalogue for this book is available from the British
Library.

This book is a work of fiction. Names, characters, places
and incidents are either a product of the author's
imagination or are used fictitiously.
ISBN: 9780957695702

Cover design by Gee Mac
Printed and bound by Lightning Source UK

To my son, Timur Doran, with much love

The Red Shoes

The time for take-off moves around on the hands of the clock. The queue is stationary; a murmur of discontent ripples toward you – Turkish officials who came over for the royal wedding have commandeered the plane. You will fly tomorrow.

People start to move away. You watch as they cross the hall and when you eventually manage to control your trolley enough to follow them, they are already circling a woman in a red hat who is giving out vouchers for an airport hotel.

You are stranded, beached by the whale that is your piled-high trolley. There are no left luggage lockers. They are all closed since the bomb scares.

The year is 1980, sometime in late July. You don't remember the exact date; you do remember it was the day after the wedding of Charles and Diana. Your aunt had dropped you at the airport entrance. She hadn't parked and come in, not this time. But she had waited, boot open, while you'd found a stray trolley and with difficulty piled your bags three high. She'd waved you goodbye and watched as you'd pushed your swaying trolley towards the Turkish Airlines check-in.

A few weeks ago you had studied your biorhythms, seen how all your luck plummeted to a trough on this day,

1

the day you were due to fly out of Heathrow; you'd dismissed it as nonsense even though someone had told you that airline pilots tracked their biorhythms, refused to fly on the days they were down.

You want to abandon your trolley with all its bags bulging with other people's desires. The reason for your huge overdraft: a Kenwood whisk that will never be used but hoarded in a bedroom drawer; washing-up liquid, two jars of Nescafé, a trilby for your father-in-law – gifts running out to the most distant of relatives. You want to cry with rage that you cannot walk out of the airport and disappear in a taxi or on a bus or the Tube into London. You cannot even go for a coffee or to the toilet.

You call your aunt, she laughs, she knows your luck runs bad with the airlines; she has been here before. You wait for her in the draught of the pickup point, watch dignitaries from the royal wedding arrive: An Arab with five wives, one who looks English, diplomats in black suits with black bags. You wonder who is sitting in your seat on their way to Istanbul.

Your aunt knows where the hotel is. You pile all your bags into the boot of her car and she takes you there; a square block of windows and concrete. You find another trolley and together you go up in the lift, along a corridor, past chambermaids and trolleys piled high with soiled sheets.

You go with your aunt to her house, sit with her at her kitchen table. You feel flat with frustration; there is a metallic taste in your mouth. You phone Istanbul and get no sympathy. The welcome meal has been cooked. All the

2

relatives have gathered. He and his brothers had waited hours at the airport.

Why didn't you come?

You explain, but it is not good enough.

Why were you so stupid as to book with that airline?

You eat lamb chops, new potatoes and salad with your aunt and her family – she says stay – she will take you to the airport in the morning. You remind her of your luggage at the hotel. Later that night, your aunt's husband drives you to the hotel.

You kiss him quickly on the cheek, and he laughs and says he might see you again tomorrow.

The corridors are empty; you feel afraid. You put your suitcases against the door, turn the lock, and are glad you did so because in the middle of the night someone tries your door. You sit propped up in bed with the light on, dozing, listening.

Next day you fly out. Your husband is there to meet you, terse and unwelcoming. Tells you how you have put his family to a great inconvenience and you lower your head and let him load the bags into the taxi. He talks to the driver. You pick up the odd word and wonder why this place feels so like coming home – the fisherman standing in his tethered boat, feet placed wide, selling his morning catch; the constant song of horns, echoes answering echoes. A skyline spiked with minarets – the air heavy with diesel fumes – the heat – and you want to stay and wander among the noise of the city. But no, you must take the ferry, take the suitcases home; enter a flat no longer prepared in welcome.

The suitcases are placed in the hall. Your mother-in-law circles them, greedy to search through all the contents; to make sure that the presents you have brought her are the best. But your husband tells her she must wait until dusk, wait for your father-in-law. You must drink black tea out of small glasses. Eat pastries of cringing sweetness. Wait until he comes, and present him with his trilby.

Ah, Mashallah, these English make such quality.

You present your mother-in-law with the Kenwood whisk. If you had one at home you would use it all the time, but she takes it, as you had guessed she would, to hide in her room; a treasure to be gloried over in the silent hours of the long afternoons. Ever since you arrived she has been mouthing secretly at you from behind the men – *Cigarettas?* – then raising her eyebrows up into her scarf, or winking at you.

No mother, your husband says. *She has not brought you any cigarettes, what would father say?*

Your husband does not know that you have two boxes of Marlborough hidden among your clothes. You will wait until the day you are leaving and then present them to her. You will part friends. If you give her the cigarettes before then, they will know it was you that brought them into the house. This woman could never buy such quality cigarettes, except from the illegal street runners across the water in Istanbul. Boys, running, catching, shouting – *Marlborough... Marlborough... Marlborough* – as insistent as a machine gun. This woman would never venture there alone.

The aunts come, sit with you and drink tea. They

4

eye you curiously, addressing you through your husband
as they wait for presents, presents that your mother-in-law
has persuaded him to let her have. You smile, nod, kiss
their hands, and serve them tea in tiny glasses. He presents
them each with a flat grey crochet hook. They grumble at
how you treat such important old ladies and he laughs, his
hand to his mouth, and asks them to forgive you for, you
see, you do not understand their ways.

The brothers come for their Lacoste polo shirts,
pulling over their heads their work-soiled T-shirts,
showing chests cushioned with black hair and their father
shouts at them for showing the women so little respect and
they take their Speedo trunks and go out onto the balcony
at the back.

Always you feel inadequate, that you have not
bought enough and yet you dread the white envelope that
you know will be waiting when you return home. You can
hear him shouting, following you around the house,

*How? How have you managed to run up such a
large overdraft?*

You could say – it is my money and I shall spend it
how I see fit. But you have learned to keep your mouth
shut.

At night you are alone, quiet in the back room of the
bottom flat. You unpack your half of a suitcase that
contains the few hard-saved, hard-sewn clothes. The thick
green washing-up liquid has leaked. It will wipe easily
from the cellophane wrapped cigarette boxes but not from
your clothes. Wash after wash will not remove the rising
suds and you will be scolded for being so wasteful with

the water. You separate the soaked clothes from the dry and there, at the bottom, is your one extravagance – a pair of blood-red leather sandals; all leather, even the wedge heel and the stalk that slots between the toes. You pick one up and smooth your hand across the grain. You place them under the bed but think better of it and put them back in your suitcase. You zip the suitcase shut and place it under the bed. Outside in the yard you hear the Alsatian that you have not yet seen, growling softly. The Imam calls, a single voice in the dark and, weary with strangeness, you sleep to be woken in the morning by your sister-in-law, Esra. At nineteen and already hurrying towards old age; a tooth missing, a belly slack from two small boys; sons to be proud of. She eyes you with envy; you are a threat, the wife of the elder son. A man-woman, an educated woman who chooses to help with the chores, who does not have to swill the yard or jump to her elders' command.

Before the heat of the day penetrates the quiet streets of wooden-slatted houses, you venture out with your husband. You carry a present that he has salvaged for the important aunt. The aunt you must visit. She thanks you curtly for the fine blanket. She wants to know what the other aunts received. Your husband explains and she smiles, toothless. You have gauged it right. She presents you with a hand-embroidered scarf.

You can wear it now - be a good Muslim woman. Mashallah.

You eat lunch at home in the courtyard. You are shaded from the sun by a vine, heavy with ripening fruit. It is strung along criss-cross wires. You try to help with the

6

serving. Your mother-in-law bids you sit. For the first three days, you are to be treated as a guest in her house and besides, she sits down opposite, you are a good girl. You stare back puzzled. She nips your arm and raises her eyebrows up into her scarf, blowing imaginary smoke rings into the air. Esra serves you meatballs, salted beans and torn bread. She has tied her scarf tight at the back of her neck. Sweat is dripping from her pale forehead, gathering in her black brows. You thank her as she pours a cool glass of water for you. She laughs and says that as her older sister, you are welcome.

The dog whimpers hot in the pit below. He is chewing something red, a bloodied bone.

After lunch you go and stand by the rail and look down at the dog.

It is not a bloodied bone.

It is a blood-red sandal.

The Sand Eggs

A wind blows. A hot wind through a city of silence.

The bones of men and boys lie perfect where they fell, white bones on yellow sand.

A city of white marble and black crows.

The searing wind blows in off a rippled sand, that was once sea.

The black-hulled boats, stranded, creak like old leather.

This once-island city of white marble, like a beached whale, lies surrounded by sand.

The only travellers through the city are five women veiled in red, a scar that travels in silence through the sand-filled streets.

The crows are silent, except for the movement of their wings: a gentle bending of bone. They hover above the fountain, watching the women who have come to bathe and quench their thirst, women who are now queens, queens of nothing.

Women who were brought as child brides from across the straits, who arrived with hennaed messages on their hands and feet. Symbols that they did not understand, symbols of their family, symbols which made their husband, the fat man with the liquorice hair, choose them.

These symbols are the only proof of who they were.

8

The Sand Eggs

Every washday they faithfully darken the fading henna; sharing hands, looking for similarities between the symbols.

Like queens the women travel the city. No longer do they bow their heads, hurry invisible among the men and the boys. They explore the rooms that until now have been forbidden to them: the temple where the men knelt in prayer, where the women, until now, could only leave offerings to the Gods on the steps outside, the library; shelves and shelves of books and only pictures that the women could understand; pictures of gold, pictures of animals and birds that they had never seen. Flowers, trees, and green landscapes that dreamlike they remember from their childhood.

The men died first. They gathered on the sand, listening, waiting, knowing, and then the wind with the heat came and the men dropped where they stood. Before nightfall, the flesh had dried from their bones; the bones that now lie on the sand; a fractured web of white on yellow.

The women took their boys and hid in the great hall. On the morning of the third day of the wind, the boys went blind, calling for their mothers with a new command in their voice. On the tenth day the wind began to drop. The women went out in search of food and the boys ignoring their mother's wishes, wandered blindly along the beach, keeping in the lee of the city; searching for the cool wind that had once come in off the sea; listening for the waves that had once gently sung them to sleep.

They found the boys at dusk, their flesh already

stripping to bone; smaller, whiter bones than their fathers.

The women worked their tongues in silence, flicking the tip off the roofs of their mouths.

Grief, or the wind, made them mute.

Early the next morning, all the women, except for the five wives of the liquorice man, had left the city, spreading out across the rippled sand, searching the horizon for their homeland. The green homeland they had seen in the books.

The five women watched them go, sifted sand through hennaed toes; a pulsing herd of red antelope moving slowly, getting smaller, nearing the horizon.

The women had never been allowed to keep their daughters. At five days old the baby girls were sent out to sea on a black-hulled boat. A cradle carefully placed among the shrimp nets and lobster pots. A five-day-old baby returning to their mother's homeland, a land of pink blossom and orchards.

Each woman would notch the year that their daughters left; keeping a conch shell wrapped in silk for each one; the symbols of their tiny left palm copied exactly onto the shell. Every spring the mother would place another notch along the serrated edge of the shell until she counted her fingers and three. Then, after thirteen years, a daughter should return to be married to a man already chosen.

Every year the boat would dock in the early morning before the sun touched the water. The young girls, a whimpering red sprawl tethered to the deck of the black-hulled boat. The girls were bathed and anointed with sandalwood, a fingertip of vermilion daubed on each forehead; their bodies scoured for birthmarks, their palms for family symbols. Each woman with a conch shell with thirteen notches would bring it to the girls, trace the markings of their palms and then the markings on the shell. They never quite matched.

The women search for a secret room under the great hall; the walls are of marble. The floor is of sand. Water seeps up through the sand. It is cool.

The women gather in the darkness. Sit silent at the heat of the day. Touching in the darkness, wet flesh, warm flesh.

The last wife, who arrived the year before, is the only woman who still carries a child in her belly. In the great hall above, the women lay out their red veils on the white marble floor. They place the girl, now in labour, on their veils. A new beginning, a daughter they can keep. They can become queens of a new land, a land of white marble, a land of hope.

The child is born, silent, still. It is a boy. The women leave the mother and carry the infant down to the sands to join the bones of his brothers. The moon is full. It has been full ever since the wind came with the heat. The wind that sucked the tide back until all around was land. The women are bare-headed. The moonlight catches their shaven heads, a punishment for stillbirth.

They wander aimlessly along the beach, searching for a sea. The sadness of the dead child hangs in the air.

The women flicker their once shrill tongues in silence aching to pour all the sadness out into the night. Just one child and they could have lived again, a child for the future. A child to build a new beginning.

Clustered under a mound of sand they find a turtle's nest. White eggs, big enough to fill clasped hands, pulse, a slight pulse, warm to the touch.

Carefully they return the eggs. Smooth the sand mound and wait, wait for the cracking of the shell, the scratching of new life, the run to the sea.

The women wait many days for the hatching of the eggs. They know instinctively that the hatching will come at night. During the day only two women stand guard, but at night they all gather on the sand, sleeping at the foot of the mound.

It comes, as they knew it would, in the night; the first cracking, the first struggle. The women take the lids off their covered baskets and wait, scooping each turtle up as it makes a dash for the sea.

The creatures, like the women, are mute. They scurry across the sand floor of the secret room. The women try to feed the turtles on dried fish, soaked in water and from the milk of the young mother. They do not eat. They scurry around the walls, all twenty-five keeping together. At night, the women each scoop five turtles into their covered baskets.

They are marked in henna, given the symbols of their adoptive mother.

The turtles will become their new children. Together in the silence they will understand each other. The turtles will stay. They will breed and every year there will be more clustered mounds of eggs buried on the beach and the women in red will be queens. The books in the library will reveal their secrets. From the pictures they will glean the meaning of the black scratches spread out like black bones on the page. They will sit cross-legged in a circle on the silk carpets of the temple, under the stained glass dome. They will become kaleidoscope queens, happy in their new freedom. They will climb the high towers and take from the crow's nests, now made of white bone, the white eggs that give the crows hope, that make them gather at the fountain, turning the white marble black; making the women wait for their bathing.

One by one, the turtles die until each woman has only two that she can place in her covered basket; take with her at night to hold as comfort in the darkness. Although it is hard flesh, it is a comfort to hold, to pretend.

The women carry the dead turtles down to where their son's bones lay and place them carefully at the edges. With each turtle that dies, hope fades.

The women place the live turtles in their covered baskets and take them down to the beach. They wait deep into the night for the appointed time. They take the covers off the baskets and tilt them so that the turtles can escape. Like a black arrow the turtles all take the same direction. They head for the ribbed sand that was once sea. The women hesitate and then together run across the ridged sand, passed the black-hulled boats, following their turtles; the mottled shells showing the ringed family symbols of each woman. As the sun rises low on the horizon it blinds the women and they bow their heads, look back at the marble city glinting, an aspect of the city they have not seen since they were thirteen years old.

The turtles follow a line across the dry straits taking the women to the land of their birth, to the land of their lost daughters.

As the day begins to fade to dusk the young girl slows, longing to return with her four mothers to the marble city. She has no daughter to seek across the wide straits; the straits that seemed so quick to cross when she came the year before on a black-hulled boat. The women slow, wait for her, staring anxiously into the distance as the turtles keep up their speed, racing, still racing for the sea.

At night the women can no longer see the turtles. The ribbed sand begins to slope gradually to a hollow, sheltering them from the wind. The moon shows the women shrimp nets and lobster pots. The fishing ground where their men had come.

At dawn the women are woken by a familiar wailing. A wailing of grief they had known all their lives until the wind came. The oldest woman is standing amongst the lobster pots, head back, flickering her tongue in and out. She points to her feet

The other women, puzzled shake their heads.

The wailing woman throws up her hands, showing hennaed palms.

The women move closer. Among the lobsterpots are baskets with handles

14

The Sand Eggs

In the baskets they see tiny frames of white ribs.
Like delicate birdcages, made for tiny songbirds.
Skulls the size of eggs lie white in the sand; the
skulls of their daughters.

The Hair of the Prophet

The child is beautiful. She will not be when she grows into full womanhood, but for now she is and I welcome her gentle smile and inquisitive ways as we follow the aunt hobbling down towards the harbour.

As we pass through the harbour gates the ferry is just docking. Its hollow hooter booming out across the bay, shaking the clarity of the early morning air. Suddenly I feel glad to be alive in spite of being captured, whisked away against my will by this strange old woman. She looks up at me; squinting through her thick glasses, she tuts, clicking her tongue against her rotten teeth.

'What does she say?' I ask Leyla.

'She says if you are a good Muslim woman, you should be wearing a scarf and raincoat like she does.'

'Why aren't you wearing a scarf and raincoat?' I ask.

'I am eleven so she doesn't bother, but soon she will want me to wear it too.'

'Will you?' I ask.

She smiles at me gently as if I am a silly child and shrugs her shoulders.

We sit out on deck and watch in silence as the ferry weaves its way through the tangle of tiny fishing boats.

The sun is already unbearably hot and my jacket and skirt, which I made hurriedly before journeying to this country, feel awkward and ill-fitting.

Today we are not disturbed by the vendors selling glasses of tea. They have fallen silent with the onset of Ramadan. Usually I spend my days within the coolness of the apartment, sleeping in the quiet of the afternoon waiting for the fall of darkness and the call of the Imam. But today I am being taken to Istanbul and the smothering heat of the city.

Leyla takes my hand and twists my rings. She smoothes the pale hollow where my wedding ring usually sits. Picking up my other hand, she turns the old gold of my wedding ring. It has a rose glow, which she finds unusual. I can see a question forming in her mind. I cannot tell her that I am married to Burak, her cousin, and that in England I live openly as his wife. His father must not find out that his eldest son has married an English woman, a cheese eater. Not yet, not until they get used to me. He may disinherit him from his lands.

I remove my hand and gently stroke her cheek, smooth the bridge of her nose, where the converging eyebrows, even now, begin to mar her beauty,

'Çok güzel.' I say. 'You are very pretty.'

The old aunt, who has been dozing, stirs and taps her walking stick on the deck, 'Bismillah.' she says, 'bismillah.'

'Do you understand?' asks Leyla.

'You say bismillah when someone says your baby is beautiful,' I reply. 'Isn't it to keep the evil eye away?'

17

Leyla smiles, 'You know a lot. You are a good Muslim!'

I know the family watch me for signs of weakness, see if I sneak a morsel of the food we must prepare for the evening meal but I feel neither hungry nor thirsty. Meal times have become just a gap in the day. The hardest time is the late afternoon when my third eye begins to thump with the beat of my heart, the hammer striking more and more heavily until, by early evening, it becomes an unbearable blindness.

When we arrive in the city the pier is thronged with people: women in dark headscarves and raincoats. Old men in trousers strangely gathered at the crotch and young men in designer outfits.

Young boys selling foreign cigarettes run and shout through the crowd. I hang on to Leyla's arm and we push our way through. The aunt is off in the distance. Her bloated legs overhanging her shoes like a hoofed animal.

At a market stall she stops. In the morning sunlight peppers glisten red and green, aubergines mahogany, but the old woman is not interested in polished aubergines or peppers varnished to enamel. She is rummaging, poking with her stick in a box on the floor.

She beckons Leyla, '*Gel!*'

The girl blushes with embarrassment and, crouching, hands her aunt two shrivelled peppers, and an aubergine that is blooming pale brown from its green hood.

'*Ne kadar?*' The old woman asks, 'How much?'

18

The stallholder scratches his cheek and replies.

'*Bah!*' she says. 'That much?'

He pleads with her, 'I have five children to raise, Haj.'

The old woman throws the aubergine and peppers back into the box and begins to shuffle off. The man comes to the front of his stall and picks up the discarded produce. He wraps them in newspaper. The aunt turns and slips a note into his hand.

'How does he know she is a Haj?' I whisper to Leyla.

'The ring on her finger, tells him that she has been to Mecca. They all respect her very much.'

This woman who, it is rumoured, has so much gold under her bed that the bed legs have to be propped on bricks, is buying old vegetables!

Leyla is handed the newspaper parcel. She puts it in her bag. I watch as the old aunt makes her way up the street in front of us hitting, with her stick, the rubbish strewn in front of her. My shoes are beginning to rub and the long sleeved, high-necked nylon blouse, a present from my mother-in-law, is now scratchy with sweat. The hum of the traffic drums in my ears. I watch fascinated as diesel fumes hover in the air.

'Where are we going?' I ask Leyla.

'My aunt is taking us on a pilgrimage. My mother says we are very lucky.'

'Yes. But where are we going?' I ask again.

'On a pilgrimage.'

'Are we walking?'

19

'I think so, maybe, unless my aunt gets tired.'

I take Leyla's arm and for a moment, close my eyes. I wish myself back at my in-laws' apartment slumbering with the great-grandmother in the coolness of the back bedroom.

For what seems like miles we push our way through crowded streets, past porters, harnessed like horses, carrying wardrobes and other huge burdens upon their backs. Until finally, the aunt comes to a halt. 'I think we will get a taxi,' she says. 'The sun is too high in the sky for an old woman to walk much further.'

And lo! and behold around the next corner is a taxi rank, a line of black Mercedes, the drivers gathered around a backgammon board on the bonnet of the first taxi. They look at Leyla and me, searching for a sign of what or who we are. I lower my eyes and expect the aunt to climb into the first taxi, but she doesn't. She haggles with the driver and when he won't agree on a price, she moves down the line until she finds a driver who is willing to be disturbed for the price she wants to pay. She climbs into the front of the taxi, and Leyla and I clamber into the back. The aunt shouts at the driver. He is smoking during Ramadan. He is not a good Muslim.

I close my eyes. The breeze from the open window is wonderful and cools my pounding head. The third eye is awake early today. I hope this journey will last forever.

Too soon, we arrive at a cobbled square shaded by high walls and trees in full leaf. At one end of the courtyard, women with covered heads swarm, chanting and swaying as they wait to enter the mosque. We join the throng. I take Leyla's arm, feeling suddenly afraid. The aunt sits down on a wall outside the huge hollow of the doorway, and Leyla kneels before her and lifts the aunt's grotesquely swollen feet, gently removing her dust-laden shoes. The aunt fumbles in her raincoat pocket and hands Leyla a bundle; a scarf and a string of prayer beads for us both.

The Mosque is heavy with the smell of warm bodies and a burning oil that is unfamiliar to me. My bare feet spread wide over the beautifully woven colours of the kilim.

Leyla tugs my arm, '*Gel!*'

We move towards the back of the Mosque where we sink to our knees. I lean my back against the wall. Leyla begins to pray. The Mosque fills rapidly and soon we are surrounded by women praying and chanting; there is no room to pray properly, so we hold our palms upwards and murmur the words:

'*Bismillah rahman al rahim.*'

'Where is your aunt?' I whisper to Leyla.

She shrugs, 'I think near the front. Near the hair.'

'What are you saying?' I ask.

'The hair of The Prophet.'

The chanting suddenly becomes louder. Leyla shakes her head at me and then lowers it in prayer. I follow suit, mimicking the mumble of the women around me. The chanting goes on and on and on. It lulls me like a gentle sea, soothing my pounding head. I want to lie down but there is no room. Behind me is the wall and to each side and to the front I am cushioned by the bodies of other praying women. Gradually the chanting slips further and further into the distance. Suddenly, my head jerks upward. I must not go to sleep. I must stay awake. I must. If I am caught sleeping what will happen? Would a fearful shrieking and wailing arise?

Allah, Allah, Allah: That terrible twisting of tongues. What would they do with this foreigner in their midst?

I must stay awake. Soon the chanting will stop. Soon it will be all over and we will be out in the fresh air. I must not go to sleep. Please God let me stay awake. I take deep breaths and twist my beads chanting over and over again words I do not know the meaning of but have learnt by heart.

The Imam's voice rises and falls, rises and falls on and on he chants. The women around me sway gently back and forth. My legs are cramped underneath me, fizzy with pins and needles. I try to shuffle them sideways and nudge accidentally, the woman next to me. She raises her head furtively. I am surprised. She is very young, very pale. Her clothes had suggested otherwise.

On and on the Imam chants. I begin to fade gently, gently, so gently into a sleep of pure luxury. Away in my own land, being myself. The Imam's voice rises to a shriek. My chin jerks onto my chest and I jolt my head upwards. I look at Leyla to see if she has noticed. She is eyeing me out of the side of her wonderful green slanting eyes. I lower my head again this time in prayer. My heart is pounding in my throat.

There is a sudden silence. I open my eyes. Slowly,

very slowly the women are moving.

We stumble to our feet. 'What happens now?' I whisper.

'We see the hair of The Prophet.' Leyla whispers, grasping my hand in excitement.

'What hair?' I ask.

'The hair of The Prophet.'

We move around the corner. At the front of the Mosque, I can see candles burning and woman prostrating themselves in front of a glass case.

It is a hair. A single strand of hair pulled taut as a violin string. It sits in a gilded glass cage illuminated by a bright spotlight. In its solitary state, it is quite beautiful.

Leyla and I do not prostrate ourselves. The Imam has become impatient, and now that the elders have gone he wants us to move quickly. To leave the Mosque we have to push our way back through the mass of woman still waiting excitedly to see the hair of The Prophet. The main door at the front of the Mosque stands open, the sunlight shafting through, but we have to return to the door at the back so that we can retrieve our shoes. I notice how many of the shoes are shabby and the curious habit these people have of caving in the backs of even the newest shoes. I prise my swollen feet into my shoes and casually remove my headscarf.

The aunt is sitting on a low round wall that circles a tree. She is deep in prayer, her thumb working the cornelian strand of beads that entwines her fingers.

Leyla smiles up at me. '*Mashallah*. We saw the hair of The Prophet.'

I breathe in the warm fresh air. A gentle breeze lifts the leaves in the tree above us. I am not sure what to do. I want to sit down on the wall next to the aunt but fear it might be seen as disrespectful. Soon, very soon, we will be going home.

The aunt squints up at us. '*Mashallah, Mashallah.*'

'*Mashallah*,' we repeat.

'*Gel*,' The old woman heaves herself off the wall and turns to walk across the courtyard.

'Where are we going now?' I ask Leyla.

'I'm not sure.'

'Are we going home?'

'I don't know,' Leyla says. She looks up at me, wondering at my questioning.

I watch the black stooped figure hobbling off into the distance. Suddenly she turns and enters through a gate in the wall.

It is a walled cemetery. All the monuments are of marble. They glisten and sparkle in the bright sunshine. The glare from them hurts my eyes and makes my head pound even more loudly. I feel sick. Saliva is beginning to pool in my mouth. I swallow hard and follow the aunt as she makes her way between the stones to a grave sheltered under the back wall. She begins to pray.

The writing on the headstone is in Arabic. I know that there cannot be any relatives buried here - all their family are buried in Trabzon.

'Who?' I ask Leyla in a whisper.

'A famous person in our history.'

The aunt visits grave after grave, Leyla and I trailing

24

behind, like little ducklings. I think to slip out and sit on the wall surrounding the tree. But how can I say I am tired when this old woman still keeps going?

It is late afternoon and the sun is dipping behind the high wall when eventually we make our way out of the graveyard. We return to the courtyard outside the Mosque, which is now busy with men washing their feet at the fountain in preparation for prayer.

I am so weary. All I want to do is lie down and sleep. Surely now, we will go home. There are taxis arriving in the square every few minutes, bringing the men, who have money, to prayer. We could step into one now. The aunt goes up to a driver and speaks to him but turns away and he leaves without us.

'Why didn't we get that taxi?' I ask Leyla.

She shrugs. 'Maybe he wanted too much money.'

I have had enough. I don't care what they think of me anymore. 'Can we go home yet?' I plead. Leyla looks at me, surprised. I try to smile. 'I have a headache.'

'My aunt may be going to prayer again at the Mosque.'

'But what about the men?'

'There is the upstairs balcony for the women.'

'*Gel.*' The aunt waves her stick at us and waddles out of the square.

I want to cry with self-pity. Cry for me wherever I am. I shouldn't ask but I do: 'Are we walking all the way back to the ferry?'

Leyla looks at me startled. She must have noted the desperation in my voice.

25

She takes my hand and raises it gently to her lips. *'Ne olduğunu?* What is the matter?'

'Nothing,' I say, feeling it is me who is the child.

After an hour of pushing our way through the crowded streets the aunt enters a shop near to the entrance of the Grand Bazaar. I have been in this shop before with my husband. It is stocked from floor to ceiling with table-cloths and soaps. The smell of mothballs and soap catches at the back of my throat and makes me feel sick again.

I recognise the people. They are kind people, distant cousins of my husband's. They greet the aunt with reverence, kissing her hand and raising it to their forehead. If it were an ordinary day they would sit us down among the bales of cloth and send for tea: clinking cups of sweet amber.

They greet Leyla and me kindly, the husband shakes my hand and his wife kisses my cheeks.

The aunt tells them where we have been. They look at me in wonder.

'Mashallah.'

The man picks up the receiver of an old black bakelite phone.

I listen. He is speaking to the aunt's eldest son. He addresses him as *Abbe*, even though he is the older man and I know that he will kiss his hand when he comes to collect us.

The eldest son does not come in person. He sends his younger brother, the man with the roaming eye. The bull red seats of the Mercedes are very hot and feel strange to our touch, like that of another skin. We sit in the

26

hooting rush hour traffic, waiting, we are all silent, even Leyla. We do not go straight to the ferry, as I had hoped, but to visit the offices of the elder son, Orhan. He wishes to pay his respects to his mother before she boards the ferry. He sits at his enormous desk, languishing back in his leather chair under the glaring blue eyes of Atatürk, but when his mother enters, as if a boy again, he comes around from behind his desk and kisses her hand.

She appears pleased by this show of respect and clucks with satisfaction as she scans the office, looking, I suspect, for signs of beverage taking, or cigarettes. Orhan Bey is known to lapse from his religious duties.

After the aunt has satisfied herself that her son is being a good Muslim, we are taken to the ferry terminus in the Mercedes, sweeping away the crowd as we arrive.

The ferry is thronged with people returning from work but we manage to squeeze ourselves onto the bench seats of the lower deck where the air is thick and stuffy and where the aunt finally succumbs to sleep. Her mouth open, hand on stick, she snores gently. Leyla looks at me with her sideways eyes and smiles. I take her hand and close my eyes. The gentle sway of the boat lulls me into a deep slumber.

I am awoken by Leyla gently shaking my shoulder. 'We have arrived.'

The aunt is sitting upright and alert as a bird. She beckons Leyla, who heaves her onto her poor swollen feet.

My head pounds like a drum. All I want is to lie down and feel the security of a mattress pressing against my back. I hope my husband will be there to meet me off the ferry. I have never before walked alone though the oleander-lined streets. I am the property of a man in this country, and his honour must be protected.

'I think I can find my way back on my own,' I say to Leyla hesitantly.

'No you mustn't,' she says. 'My aunt is going to cook for us; we will break our fast with her.'

'But how will they know, at home, where I am?'

'It is already arranged. I am not sure, maybe they will join us for our meal.'

I know this will not be so. Burak will not pass up his mother's cooking for his aunt's, whose cooking with the cheap oil is legendary.

We crawl slowly up the hill. The aunt huffs, stopping frequently to pull her headscarf tighter around her head. The sun is now low in the sky and there is a faint breeze from the sea.

When we enter the house, the aunt goes immediately to prayer, while Leyla goes to the kitchen to prepare the vegetables.

'Can I help?' I ask wearily.

She puts down the knife she has been using to top the okra, and takes my hand.

'*Gel.*' Come.

She leads me to a small bedroom, just inside the front door. The bed is covered by the most exquisite royal blue velvet quilt.

'Is this your aunt's bed?' I ask.

'Yes.' She says. 'But she won't mind if you want to have a rest.'

'I'll just have five minutes.' I say. 'Then I'll come and help in the kitchen.'

She laughs, and kissing me gently on the forehead, closes the door.

I look to see if the bed legs are firmly on the ground but they are covered by the quilt and I am too weary to lift the cover to see if the legend of the gold is true.

I am woken by Leyla stroking my hair. She is wearing a long white gown and looks like a tawny angel smiling down at me. I sit up. The sunshine outside is bright. I am confused. 'What time is it?'

Leyla shows me her watch; 10 o'clock. I look outside; it is bright sunshine. I don't understand and then slowly the truth dawns. I have slept through a whole night and not broken my fast. Now I must live through another whole day without food or water.

'Why didn't you wake me?' I wail.

She laughs. 'We tried to but you were too deep in sleep.'

'Burak came and he tried, but nothing would wake you. *Mashallah*. We tried again before dawn but you were like a dead person. My aunt said that the call of the Imam would wake you but it didn't.'

I sit on the edge of the bed. My clothes are crumpled and damp with sweat. My head is thumping.

When I enter the living room the aunt looks up and cackles. '*Mashallah*.'

'Tell your aunt I am sorry I took her bed.'

'It is not a problem,' Leyla says. 'You are our

guest.'

I stand by the open window and look out down the narrow street to the sea sparkling in the distance. I feel like a prisoner held here against my will.

'Can we phone Burak to come and get me?' I say.

'But you are staying with us today,' exclaims Leyla. 'Burak has gone to the city with his father.'

'I have to go back,' I hear myself say. 'I will go on my own if you give me directions.'

'What is the matter?' The aunt asks. Leyla translates for her and she laughs.

'She says you are a funny person,' Leyla says, looking at me with a puzzled expression.

She walks me back through the narrow dirt streets of unpainted wooden clapperboard houses. The only shade is from the oleander trees whose pink flowers are wilting in the heat. Leyla leaves me at the door of the apartment block and skips off back down the street.

I climb the marble stairs to the first floor. The door of the apartment is slightly ajar, empty shoes spilling out into the hall. Everything is still. I am alone. No one is waiting my return. They have all gone about their daily business. I suddenly wonder why I was so desperate to return.

In the small bedroom at the back of the apartment, I hear a faint murmur. It is the grandmother praying quietly to herself. She looks up and nods, her walnut face filling with pleasure. I sit down next to her on the cool linoleum floor and, taking her gnarled and hennaed hand, raise it to my lips.

She is the only woman of this family who wants Burak to take me as his wife.

She strokes my hair.

We sit quietly at peace and await the dusk.

Billy

I shall call him Billy; a ninety-year-old child with a head as purple and transparent as an un-feathered fledgling. He lay prostrate on the pavement, tiny in his dark pin-stripe suit. Big boots, I remember he wore big, black boots; proper, polished, workmen's boots.

Holding Billy's hand was a man in shorts. The man had a child with him, a boy of seven or eight wearing a Sheffield Wednesday shirt. The man crouched down on the pavement and held Billy's hand, letting him cling tight.

A woman with short tinted hair, a cleaner at one of the local schools I think, on the way to see her mother, knelt behind Billy. She stroked between his shoulder blades with one hand and cushioned his shoulder from the pavement with the other – all the while speaking words, soft, soothing words of comfort.

Billy was on the pavement outside my house; well, just a little way along. I was going for a paper when someone shouted, 'Ring an ambulance will you, love?'

I saw the crown of an old head and people crouching. The woman on the other end of the phone asked me if he was an elderly gentleman. I should have asked 'Why?' but I didn't. I said 'I think so.'

I rushed upstairs and got a blanket and a pillow, though it was a hot day and Billy had on a pin-stripe suit.

The man holding his hand said, 'I think he's warm

32

enough.'

'I've brought a pillow,' I said.

The man shook his head, 'I've already put my travel rug under his head. I think he's okay, thanks.'

He put his mouth close to Billy's ear. 'Can you hear me, love? What's your name?'

He looked up at me, 'Billy...I think he said... Billy.'

I put my pillow and blanket on the bonnet of a car and crouched down at the back of Billy's head. There was a woman standing behind the man who held his hand. She had a wide flat face and shoulder-length curly blonde hair. On her hip she balanced a small child. She had parked her grey jeep on the side street that ran up the hill behind us. It was her that had seen him fall, who had left her child strapped in, and run to Billy, now quiet on the pavement.

'He just sort of crumpled,' she said, 'as he came down the hill. He seemed to be moving awful fast.'

My legs were beginning to cramp, crouched there at the top of Billy's head. I felt helpless, scared, hoping he wouldn't die before the ambulance came. A tall man in a royal blue shirt off on an early night out had also called an ambulance. He was someone who I felt we should have known, maybe an ex-footballer. He had stopped, parked his big car on the other side of the road and dialled 999 on his mobile phone.

We were all held there suspended in time, whether by curiosity or compassion or a mixture of both. We had to stay. We had to wait for the ambulance. No one knew Billy. We asked passers-by. They shook their heads. No one had ever seen him in the club at the end of the road. I'd never seen him pass my window as I had seen other men; men suddenly retired and falling slowly every year into death. No one knew Billy, not even the cleaner lady, or Cyril who passed my window three or four times a day with his nearly-blind white stick, his cap and his 'getting away from the wife' walk.

Billy held his suited arms tight across his chest and when the man holding his hand tried to slip his free hand inside Billy's breast pocket, he seemed to pull them tighter; tight as a vice around his chest.

'What's your name, old lad? Is it Billy?'

Billy lay silent on the pavement. I could see all the fine veins on the top of his head; fine red and blue threads like the head of a foetus illuminated in the womb. Above his ear and on the top of his head were yellow encrustations where he must have knocked himself, maybe on an earlier fall.

A group of kids gathered on the corner. I wanted to tell them to bugger off.

The man holding Billy's hand looked up, 'Clear off!' He mouthed, 'Go on, get lost.'

I looked at his son, who stood there on one leg, 'If you want to get off....' I said.

'No' he said,' I'll wait. The ambulance should be here soon.'

It was a hot day at the end of August. Five o'clock in the afternoon. We were all in our summer clothes, except for Billy. The cleaner woman, on the way to see her mother, rubbed between Billy's shoulder blades. 'It's strange no one knows him. What's he doing up here, and dressed so smart as well?'

The woman with the child on her hip frowned, 'I saw him coming up my street when I was still in the house. He was going at a fair old lick. He must have been lathered in those clothes, the street being so steep an' all.'

'Where does that street go?' asked the man holding Billy's hand.

The woman shook her head. 'Nowhere, just the cemetery wall at the top, but you can't get through.'

'Do you think he could have been going to a funeral?' I asked.

People passing in cars on their way home looked at us, gathered, crouching on the pavement.

The ambulance came up past the club, blue light silently flashing. No siren for Billy. I waved but they had already seen us; a flock of sheep protecting the injured. Billy wouldn't let go of the man's hand. He's still breathing, the ambulance man told us. We'd known that. They went and fetched a metal trolley with wheels and between them they lifted Billy, eyes still closed, light as a child, onto the trolley.

'Can I have me hand back, mate?' the man asked. Billy let go, eyes still tight shut. The cleaner woman shook her squashed hand. The gravel from the pavement had pressed dents into the back of her fingers.

No one got in the back with Billy. We all shook our heads when they asked if anyone knew him. The ambulance men shut the doors.

The tartan rug lay folded into a pillow on the pavement. The man who had been holding Billy's hand, picked it up. It was sodden with blood, soaked through to the pavement.

'Get us a plastic bag from the car, lad.' he said to his son. The boy brought back an insulated freezer bag. I knew it was the wrong one.

'I'll get you a bag.' I said.

'No, it doesn't matter.' the man said, putting the blanket in the bag, trying not to touch the blood.

'Would you like to come in and wash your hands?'

The man looked at me, hesitated, 'No, I'll be alright.'

'Would you like me to put the bag in my wheely bin?'

'If you don't mind.'

The gathering split, going once again in invisible directions. I put the blanket in the empty wheely bin and, for a week, every time I went to the bin, I thought of Billy, and his blood lying in the bottom.

I didn't want a dog licking Billy's blood off the pavement so I filled a bowl with warm water and washing-up suds and splashed it onto the spot. It stayed. A sticky mass which, over the days, turned to a dark brown stain on the pavement.

Every time I go that way now I see that stain and think of those people and that splintered ball of human kindness, and of Billy. And wonder if, this time, he made it all the way to the cemetery.

Babaanne

The old woman clucks her tongue and claws at my white cotton sleeve for the peach that I am trying to peel for her.

Erin laughs at me.

'What is wrong?' I ask.

He laughs again, his high pitched, girlish laugh, jiggling his belly under his T-shirt. 'She says you are cutting the peel too thick, and that you are a very wasteful woman.'

He laughs again, twitching his blue plastic fly swatter at the stray flies that come in through the open window. I look at the old woman and see the faintest twinkle in her hooded black eyes. Placing the plate with the peach onto her lap, I wipe my hands then take her brown claw-like hand, oiled and stained with henna. I raise it to my lips and then to my forehead. Her fingers are long and bent towards the palm, the nails thick and coloured to stained marble. She shakes her head at me and with her free hand, gives me back the plate.

'What is the problem now?' I ask Erin.

'You haven't taken out the stone.'

I hand the plate to Erin, 'Please?'

'Bah! I'm not a woman,' he says, thrusting the plate back at me.

'Please' I plead, folding my arms tight.

I sit down at the foot of the bed where the old

37

woman sits cross-legged. From the next room come the loud snores of my mother-in-law taking her afternoon nap. Outside it is silent except for the faint drone of flies. The curtain flaps gently, streaking the intense afternoon sun across the blue linoleum floor. I watch as Erin deftly pares the gleaming flesh from the rutted stone and see the juice seep between his plump fingers.

I laugh.

'Bah!' he says, thrusting the plate roughly at his grandmother.

She cackles.

He heads for the inner door, holding his hands in front of him.

'Erin?' I call quietly, 'Where are you going?'

He puts his head back around the door, 'To wash my hands, of course.'

'Will you come back please?'

'Why?'

'I want you to ask Babaanne to tell us a story.'

He grins showing his dirty crooked teeth.

The old woman looks up from her task when she hears her name. The juice is running down the cleft in her chin. She claws at her white headscarf, staining it with pale yellow rings that gradually spread out and fade to white. I hand her the damp flannel that I have used to clean my hands.

'*Ne olduğunu?*' she croaks. 'What is it?'

I laugh and take the plate from her lap. She grimaces back in a half smile, her one black tooth hanging like a talon. I stretch and settle back to wait for Erin, listening to the water as it drains down the gully in the bathroom.

Erin is my brother-in-law; he is fifteen, with a big blubbery body and soft pink cheeks. He is a gentle boy who I sometimes make cry when I tire of his puppy-like devotion. This morning he cried when I told him to cease his chatter and now, ashamed of my cruelty, I am trying to be nice. I feel at ease when alone with him and the grandmother. They are the only two in this family that I feel truly like me.

Erin bustles back into the room, wiping his hands on his T-shirt, he tells the old woman what I have said. She slumps back on her pillow and sighs. Holding her hands out, palms upwards, she murmurs, praying to herself.

'She is praying for her dead husband and ten dead children.' Erin says, plumping himself down self-importantly next to me on the bed.

'Ask her to tell us about where she was born,' I whisper.

The old woman pulls at her white headscarf. The purple flowers embroidered around the edge dangle into her face. Can it be true that she has lived one hundred and four years? Her skin is like setting toffee, tilting to one side, the brown creases lapping in folds to her jaw. Against her ancient skin, the white headscarf looks girlish and out of place.

Her voice croaks quietly.

'I was married at thirteen.' Erin says, translating with a smirk.

'My people were farmers. My father had a farm halfway up the mountain.'

Erin gets up off the bed and starts to skip clumsily around the room, his flip-flops slapping noisily against the lino, giggling as he flicks away imaginary flies with his swatter.

'Shut up Erin,' I hiss.

He stops, his hand still held above his head and looks at me. Two tears, one from each eye, trickle down his soft cheeks.

I stand up from the bed, take his upper arm and pull him down on the bed next to me. 'I'm sorry, but I want to hear what Babaanne has to say.'

The old woman, who has been talking all this time, stops and looks at Erin.

She shouts something at him.

'What does she say?' I ask.

He shrugs his shoulders.

I laugh, 'She says you're a big girl, doesn't she?'

'I thought you couldn't understand our language?' He looks at me curiously.

'I can't. But I know that *kız* means girl.'

Tears well up in his eyes again. 'I thought you were my friend.'

'Oh Erin, I am. It's just... I wanted to hear Babaanne tell us her story.'

The old woman is silent. She sits cross-legged on her bed. In her hands, she holds a string of plump beads the colour of dark honey. She rubs each one in turn between her forefinger and thumb, each one a different prayer.

Erin flounces off the bed, 'I'm tired of this. You ask her.'

I cross the lino and sit on the edge of her bed. Erin sits down on the empty bed and leans back on his elbows, 'She's praying now. You'll have to wait ages.'

As if the old woman understands him she stops and takes my hand in hers, '*Mashallah*.'

'What does she mean?'

Erin smiles, 'She likes you very much.'

I put my arm carefully around her shoulders and feel the bones brittle under her thin blouse. Her scarf slips to the back of her head revealing wisps of carrot-coloured hair. She pushes me aside and pulls her headscarf forward, wrapping it tightly around her head. Her beads fall with a tinkling rattle to the lino. I bend and pick them up, cupping the warm amber in my hands. They are as smooth and rounded as pebbles. The string that holds them together, I notice, is a gold chain. I place them back in her skirted lap.

'It is good they were not broken.' Erin says, 'They have been in our family for generations. They are very valuable.'

I tug at the pale green bed cover, smoothing it flat with my hand, 'They are very beautiful. Where did they come from?'

Erin addresses his grandmother. She picks up the beads, holding them in the light.

'What does she say?'

'She says our ancestors were cloth merchants. One of them brought them back from Persia.'

'Yes, but how long ago?' I ask.

'How should I know? How should Babaanne know? She can't even read and write.'

'Was it before the Armenian uprising?'

Erin pulls a face at me and asks Babaanne. The old lady rocks back and forth.

'Many, many, years before then,' he says.

'Ask her if she will tell us about the uprising?'

He sighs and flumps his shoulders, 'It is too hot.'

'Please, Erin.'

'Will you send me a watch like you brought my elder brother when you get back to England?'

'Would you like that?'

He grins, his cheeks pouching up under his eyes.

'Erin, don't you ever wash your teeth?'

The tears are there again. He pulls his arm angrily across his face.

His grandmother laughs, '*kız,*' she shouts,' *kız.*'

Erin struts out of the door.

I would follow him but the Grandmother catches my arm and shakes her head.

We sit in silence, her hand reptilian on my arm. I can hear the water splashing in the bathroom.

Erin comes back in and bares his teeth at me. 'There. Better?' A fly comes in through the curtains. He picks up the swat.

'I'm sorry, Erin. I didn't mean to be rude. It's just… you have such a nice face it seemed a shame to spoil it with dirty teeth.'

He shrugs. He has the shoulders for shrugging.

'Don't forget about my watch.'

'Come and tell us the story then.'

The old lady, head tilted back, is looking at us down the line of her nose, 'What is it?' she asks Erin. 'What are you saying?'

He tells her. She nods and picks up her beads, 'I was married at thirteen and I had thirteen children; unlucky, very unlucky. First I lost my husband and two of my sons to the Russians, and then two years later I lost all of my sons, except for your father.' She nods at Erin. 'Ten of my sons killed by the Armenians.'

I hiss at Erin, he looks up.

'I thought you said she had ten children before?'

He shrugs again, 'I don't know. I am just repeating what Babaanne says.'

'Are you?' I raise my eyebrows.

He snorts, 'You forget. She can't read. She can't count. How was she to know how many children she had?'

'Ask her to go on.'

Erin sighs, 'She is going on, but I can't listen to you both so you must be quiet. Just listen…'

'They nearly got me and my daughter,' she says, 'but we hid under a bridge, knee deep in water for two days. We saw them killing our neighbour. Big-bellied with child she was. Killed her and the child with the fork we used for gathering the hay.'

The old woman looks first at Erin and then at me. There is a look of pride there. Pride for having survived, not sadness for those who had not.

A fly rests on the lino. Slap, Erin brings the swat

down. The fly rises to the ceiling. I snatch the swat out of his hand.

'What?'

'Can't you just put that thing down? We are trying to talk here.'

'No we're not. I'm talking. Babaanne is talking. You're listening. And I want my fly swat back.'

'No.'

He pushes open the curtains and goes out onto the balcony. The sunlight floods into the room. The Grandmother shouts words after him that I know are swear words. I close the curtains. She beckons me to the bed. She is asking for something. I can't understand her. Erin pokes his head in through the curtains, 'Water. She wants water. I thought you understood our language?'

'Do I get it from the tap, or from the fridge?'

He shrugs, 'Tap will do.'

There is one single brass tap in the kitchen. I struggle to turn it on. The water comes suddenly gushing out, wetting me all down my front.

I hold the glass to her lips. She slurps it from the rim. She lets me hold the glass, enjoying being waited on. She nods at me and smiles.

I pass carefully through the curtains. Erin has turned pink. 'Would you like some water?' I ask.

'Not from the tap, no.'

'But Erin, I've just given some to Babaanne. Is it not safe?'

'Of course, very safe, just that it's not cold enough for me. I like mine from the fridge.'

When I get back with his water Erin is lying down on the bed swatting imaginary flies. The grandmother is playing with the purple embroidered flowers on the edge of her shawl. I sit next to her, my feet cold on the lino, 'Go on then Erin.'

He sighs, 'Why? Don't you know all this already?'

'I know some of it. I just wanted to hear about Babaanne's daily life, when she was young.'

Babaanne shakes her head at Erin and asks him what I am saying. She takes my hand. 'My father had a farm half way up the mountainside. We had two cows. My sister Esme and I would take the cows down to the lower pastures. We would stay all day, taking our lunch with us.'

Babaanne falls silent and gazes down at her upturned hands. Using her thumb from her right hand she strokes the fleshy part of her palm of her other hand, where the henna has stained darker.

'What did you take for your lunch?' Erin chides.

'You fat child,' she croaks. 'You donkey.'

The old woman lies back on her pillows and closes her eyes.

'Now look what you've done, Erin.'

'What?'

'You've upset Babaanne.'

'No, I haven't. She's useless anyway. She never tells us what we want to hear.' He swats at another fly.

'Erin, stop it.'

'What?'

'Flicking that fly swatter. It doesn't do any good.'

He juts his chin out and continues flicking. We hear

movement in the room next door: bedsprings creaking. Babaanne sits up alert as a weasel. My mother-in-law bustles her weight into the room, coughing, and scraping back her poor, flat hair under her tightly pulled headscarf.

The grandmother looks at her and sniffs. 'I can smell cigarette smoke. You whore-woman, I will tell my son.'

My mother-in-law picks the beads up from the bed, 'What are these doing here?' she asks.

Babaanne looks at me, 'Give them to the girl.'

'Why?' My mother-in-law shakes her head.

'I want her to have them.'

Erin slaps his hand with the fly swat, '*Mashallah.*'

His mother snatches the fly swatter from him, lunging at him with it, *'kız.'* she shouts, *'Like a girl.* You stay in the house with the women.'

Scuttering the Pebbles

Hilda breathes in, pulling the salt air into her nostrils and down into her lungs. She closes her eyes and listens to the sounds of the cove; the sea, gentle now, the gulls on the headland. The winter sun warms her through, comforts her whole body. The slate slab on top of the low garden wall has been soaking in the sun all day and is now as hot as an oven. Hilda presses her palms into the warmth and lets out a long, soft moan.

She turns to look up at the bedroom window and the green damask curtain fluttering through the open gap. She should return to the sick room, sit quietly in the chair by the bed; watch death creep nearer, taking its toll hour by hour on the life of her little sister, her skin yellowing like an old lampshade. But first she must sit here and take strength from the sun. If only she could stay forever, locked away from the outside world in this vale of sadness. She could wrap a shawl around the cove and the village; make her sister well. They could be young again, start life from here. She won't let her die. She will fight it. Then they can live here by the sea. Listen to its story as the year unfolds: the winter gales, the lull of the waves in summer singing them to sleep through the open window. She sighs deeply.

'That was a deep one.'

Hilda shields her eyes against the sun and looks up

47

at Peggy who has come silently to stand beside her.

'I was just thinking, Peggy, sitting here, how you can actually feel the sadness. It's like being wrapped in a protective cloak. Hidden like a small child under your mother's winter coat. I can't understand why my sister never told me of this place.'

Peggy wraps her arms around her body, and sits down beside her. 'It's lovely, isn't it? I couldn't live anywhere else and besides, if I left, I couldn't take my healing powers with me. I need to stay here to soak up the energy to make people well again. Or to give people the strength to die.'

'I wonder why other people's sadness should feel so exquisite?' Hilda says.

'It's feelings, and any feelings are better than no feelings. We're sucking away at their feelings, living off them like the bee does the pollen.'

Hilda frowns. 'Does that mean one day it will all be gone?'

'It's been here a long time, ever since the men were lost at sea.' She looks out towards the horizon. 'And don't forget, folks keep bringing their own sadness here, like you for instance.' She wipes her hands down the front of her checked overall. 'I've come to see Mary.' She nods her head up at the bedroom window. 'Not so good today is she? I've been feeling it all day.'

Hilda studies Peggy's face; her skin which is usually plump and blooming with good health, today seems to be drawn and ghost-like. Her hair, pulled back into a soft bun at the nape of her neck, usually so luxuriant, today looks so thin that Hilda can see her scalp. She must be eighty if she's a day. Hilda shakes her head. 'No, she isn't so good. I thought, we both thought, coming here might make her better. Is there nothing you can do to make her well again, Peggy?'

Peggy stands up and leans against the wall next to Hilda. 'I don't think she came here to get well. She told me she came here to die. She's comfortable here ....'

'Why? Why would she want to die here, away from all her family and friends?'

'Because,' Peggy pauses.

'You cured her last time,' Hilda says.

'She wasn't staying here, then.'

'Are you saying you could save her if I moved her over to Port Gaven?'

Peggy shakes her head. 'I think she wants to die more than she wants to live.'

Hilda turns. 'You mean you want her to die – to feed into the sadness that you live off.'

'It would be your sadness, not hers,' Peggy says. 'And you'll be leaving, taking it with you, won't you?'

Hilda bridles. 'I could decide to come and live here.'

'Where? There's only the holiday cottage you're staying in and my house that is habitable.' Peggy crosses her arms. 'Have you ever considered why you want her to live?'

'We are sisters. I love her. We share the same history. We have been grown from the same plant, I have no one else.'

49

'You're strong; you'll make a new history. Let her die here. Could you think of a better place?'

'You make it sound so very simple,' Hilda says bitterly.

'It is, my dear. If your sister really wants to live I can help her. I cured an aunt of mine and she was as far gone as your Mary. I keep seeking out that hand that will help me pull her back, but it isn't there. I'm sorry.'

Hilda gets up from the wall. 'Then I'd rather you didn't go in to see her, maybe she can fight it better without you.'

'I have to go and see her,' Peggy says calmly. 'She is my closest friend.'

'Why? So that you can add to your blanket of sadness? Keep her here forever?'

'You think it's me with the selfish motives. You can't boss her any more. She is at last making a stand. Like I said before, it wouldn't be her sadness. She would be happy here.'

Hilda sits back down on the wall and to her mortification begins to cry. 'I thought you were a healer. I thought she was your friend. Some friend!'

Peggy shakes her head. 'You have to trust me in this; I'll do my best. But remember it is her wishes I'm meeting, not yours. Now let me go and see her.'

Hilda makes to get up from the wall, 'I'll take you up.'

Peggy stays her hand. 'You wait here; enjoy the sunshine while you can.'

Hilda watches as Peggy slowly mounts the slate

steps to the house. Her skirt is grasped at the front and she can see the plump, white roundness of her bare calves. How can such an ordinary woman have such extraordinary healing powers?

The front door closes. She turns back and again looks over to the headland, shading her eyes against the lowering sun. She hears Peggy drop the latch on the bedroom door and the dull thud of the sash window as it hits the frame. Closed out, shut out, she feels a strange mixture of resentment and relief. It fills her with a restlessness, taking her from her seat on the wall, across the path and down to the fresh water stream cradled in a gully of slates, packed tightly as playing cards where only the pennywort and fern can take foothold. Hilda sees how the stream glistens black, reflecting the slate walls. She looks up, and for the first time studies the shape of the valley leading inland; she has never followed the stream before. It disappears under the road and re-emerges in the walls of an old fish yard, a store now used for upended rowing boats. She crosses the bridge and makes her way through the yard to a gate stencilled into a blackened wall, smudged with yellow lichen. Beyond the gate, Hilda can see a meadow with steep green sides running down to a meandering line of willows and alders that trace the route of the stream.

The meadow is a haven of sunlight and calm, the breeze from the sea does not reach this far up. Hilda sees that at the narrowest point of the stream is an old wooden bridge. She runs, she can't remember the last time she ran, down through the wet grass to the bridge.

She leans on the rail and looks into the depths of the stream. She can make out her reflection, her grey cropped hair, her gaunt face. She pulls a twig from an overhanging branch and throws it into the stream to break the mirror. She remembers the times she played pooh sticks with Mary, how she always had to win. Soon, maybe tomorrow, maybe next week, she will stand here and her sister will be dead, buried in the churchyard over at Bodinnick as she had requested. Will she feel able to stay, or will she want to be gone, back up country, an old woman in a semi on a grey street in a grey town?

Two years ago, when her sister's husband died, she had thought her life would get better. That she and her sister would return to their old roles, she the elder and her sweet sister Mary, as ever, bending to her whims.

Mary had been diagnosed with cancer twenty years ago and had then subjected herself to the hospital regime. Her husband had insisted. Told her she would be selfish not to. And Hilda, for once, had agreed with him. But this time, as soon as the cancer returned, Hilda had seen a different Mary, a Mary in charge of her own life. She'd come down here to Port Wynne and rented the cottage that she had dreamt of staying in ever since her first visit. Year after year her husband had booked them into a comfortable hotel over at Port Gaven and every day of their holiday, come rain or shine, Mary and her husband would come down to Port Wynne; he to fish off the rocks, she to wander amongst the rock pools and up in the village, wallowing in the tangible sadness that lay like a mist in the cove.

Mary had told Hilda all this on the train down, it spilled out of her; how she had met Peggy and how they became friends, never writing but always, once a year, during Mary's two-week holiday, fitting together like two halves of a shell, digging together in Peggy's garden, harvesting the runner beans that hung tucked away behind wide flat leaves.

And how, nearly every day, Peggy would have a visitor. A stranger standing at the gate, waiting for Peggy to turn and see them, then silently follow her into the house and sometimes a mother would bring a child and the mother would sit with Mary while Peggy took the child into the house. And she explained how these mothers would never talk of why they'd come, but sit perched on the garden bench in their Sunday best and discuss the garden or the weather or the fact that Mary wasn't from around here, was she?

She told of the summer, twenty years ago, when she had her treatment, she herself had become one of the visitors, wearing a scarf to cover her pink scalp. She had waited, clutching the top of the gate waiting for Peggy to turn.

Peggy told her that she'd been waiting for her coming. And every day of her holiday, while her husband fished off the rocks, Peggy had clasped Mary's hands between hers and day by day they fought the cancer. She stayed three weeks that summer; told her husband she would stay with Peggy and come home on the train.

Until then, Hilda had known nothing of Port Wynne, or Mary's friendship with Peggy, and when Mary had finally brought her here she had felt slighted that her own sister had told her nothing of this beautiful deserted fishing village filled with the sadness of fisherman's widows, whose men had all gone fishing and never returned; a sadness that lay just below the breastbone. She likened it to studying a beautiful painting, or a sculpture of bodies rounded and smooth as pebbles. Sadness was different to loneliness. Sadness could be beautiful. These women's lives had been made special by their mass widowhood. Unlike her own life: a headmistress, revered but not loved, no man, no place to belong to until she came here, a place that for years her own sister had kept from her.

Hilda watches fascinated as her tears drop into the stream.

The wind is up. The kitchen window rocks gently in its frame and the Rayburn damper clanks from the wind caught in the chimney. Hilda places three deep bowls of steaming pea and ham soup on a wooden tray and carries them upstairs. The sun has gone down behind the headland, dusk and a falling light of mauve fill the room.

Mary tries to sit up. 'I don't want the light on.'

Hilda places the tray on top of the chest of drawers. 'I wasn't going to turn it on.'

'I'm sorry.' Mary stretches out a hand of yellow bone and Hilda takes it, squeezing it gently as she tugs her up to a sitting position. Picking up the three crumpled pillows one by one she plumps them back into shape and places them face up showing the embroidered corners with maids in bonnets amidst lupins.

She eases Mary back onto the stacked pillows. 'Do you remember when mother embroidered these pillow cases?'

Mary smiles. 'I always remember Mother embroidering, feet tucked under her and working by the light at the side of her chair. I always thought she did these especially for me.'

'Why should she have?'

'I think it was her way of a little joke, you know the nursery rhyme:

Mary, Mary quite contrary,
How does your garden grow?
With silver bells and cockle shells,'

'And pretty maids all in a row.' Peggy finishes, switching her knitting needles over.

Hilda tugs at the embroidered corner of the pillow, 'I don't see any bells or cockleshells. Why do you always make out that it was you that was mother's favourite? Her blue-eyed girl.'

Mary sighs, closes her eyes. 'I didn't mean anything by it. It was just a fancy of mine. My way of remembering mother.'

Hilda looks across at Peggy who has paused in her knitting. She lifts one of the bowls of soup from the tray and carries it across to her. Peggy tucks her knitting down the side of her chair and without a thank you takes the soup.

Hilda places the tray on Mary's lap and lifts her own bowl from the tray. 'You need to eat something to build you up.'

'I don't want to be built up. Peggy has eased my pain, now all I want is to die in peace. To become part of this place, one of the women.'

'What an earth are you going on about? You are not going to die. Peggy is going to cure you. You can't be one of its women anymore than I can.'

Peggy speaks from the other side of the bed. 'Ah, but that's where you're wrong. For, unlike us, Mary is a widow.'

Hilda watches as her sister slowly stirs her soup, observing how the cream forms an inner and an outer circle of soft white. The room is nearly dark, the wind still rattling at the windows.

'I am fed up with fighting this cancer. I have had my life.' Mary turns to her friend. 'Go on, Peggy, continue with the story.'

Peggy places her soup bowl on the bedside table and turns towards the window, 'No rain tonight; it was said there was no rain the night of the storm that took all the men of Port Wynne.'

Hilda lifts the tray from Mary's lap, 'Why do you want to hear the same tale over and over?'

Mary turns on her side and gently rubs the embroidered corner of the pillow between her thumb and forefinger. 'Because I want to be part of it.'

Every evening since they arrived here, like a child being told a bedtime story, Mary has asked Peggy to relate the tale.

The room is almost dark. Hilda can only just make

out the forms of her sister and Peggy. Tonight, for the first time, she can hear the faint click of knitting needles, as if the knitter or knitters are in another room, and if she is not mistaken there is an overwhelming smell of fish and lanolin. She sits down in the nursing chair by the window, looks across the room trying to make out the shapes of Mary and Peggy. She senses rather than sees Peggy fumbling down the side of her chair for her knitting, tucking a needle under each arm, and then again the slow insistent click of wooden knitting needles, but in the room this time.

'They was only supposed to have gone for a night's mackerel fishing. I think some of the women feared the worst from the first morning when they didn't return. It was a daft man that decided the crew should go out that night, but once one of them had decided they were going, no man would lose face by saying he thought different, and so they sailed off around the headland. It was dusk and the sky was a hard dull grey, as were the waves that came crashing into the cove. That was the last any of the women folk ever saw of their men. If the women hadn't been stood watching, maybe, just maybe they would have turned back. But it would have taken a courageous man to turn back and face the women's ridicule. These weren't soft women. They were women brought up on hardship; hard work, that's all they knew, gutting and salting mackerel, raising children, tending their gardens.

'By eight o'clock the next morning all the women had gathered at this house, the only house in the cove that looks out to sea. They sat huddled round the fire with the shutters open, looking out; eight women and one young girl, Margaret Pascoe, who they sent up onto the headland to keep a better watch. They knitted, and waited. No one spoke, just the soft clunk of wooden needles and rough hands on oiled wool. They waited all day and as darkness began to close in, Ruth Pascoe, the girl's mother, started to weep. One of the older women spoke tersely to her, said she knew she were young but at least her child was still with her. She had two sons as well as a husband out there. That started them all off. Ruth climbed up the cliff path to the headland to collect her daughter. It was nearly dark, but it was a clear night and she could see the sea below her clear as glass. Why had they not waited just one more night? When she got back, the women all turned to her, silently begging for good news.

'Some folk over at Port Gaven spread rumours. Believed the men had crossed the Atlantic and made a new life in America, got new, younger wives. The vicar from Bodinnick came down three weeks later, said they'd found some wreckage but no bodies. Said he would come again if they found bodies, but he never did.

'They limped on for months, growing beans and fishing off the rocks. All the boats had gone, gone with the men. No one came to the village to help the women, not after the first few weeks; a village full of widows. The women over at Port Gaven wouldn't let their men near, as is the meanness of comfortable women. It was October when the men were lost, it couldn't have happened at a worse time. Winter newly upon them and that first year was a bad one. The snow was so high that the lanes were blocked for six weeks. Everyday at dusk they gathered at this house, waiting and whispering for their men. Gradually, over time, one by one, they left, all except for Ruth Pascoe. I think it was a comfort to the other women that she stayed behind.

Hilda closes her eyes; from behind her eyelids she can see the fisherwoman gathered in the room. They are stout women with wind-burnt skin and straggled hair, except for a younger woman, who is slender with an exquisite softness of features. Two of the women are sitting on the windowsill, three kneeling on the floor, three sit on the bed. There is a fire in the hearth. Ruth Pascoe, it must have been Ruth, she is the youngest woman, pushes open the storm shutters. The last of the winter sun is glinting far out at sea. They sit in silence, knitting. Under her breath Ruth is praying, begging that soon that very night they will see small black spots on the horizon that will turn into the heads of tired men and boys, and as night creeps into the cove, so also will their men.

'Gradually the village became silent, chimneys stopped smoking, dogs stopped barking, the washing lines blew limp in the wind. They all left one by one except, as I said, Ruth Pascoe. Ruth was known in these parts as a healer, like her mother before her, and her mother before her, so she managed to live off the offerings that people brought her. It's the only reason most folks came. She stayed in this house with her small daughter, Margaret, and waited all her life. Really she was the only one who had any chance of re-marrying. A fisherman from Port Gaven was sweet on her but she wouldn't have him. Some say it was because he used to row in around the headland and into the cove instead of coming over by road, so that every time she saw him bending to his oars she was reminded of her Paul, lost at sea.

He brought her fish and firewood. She would stand there in that window at night, naked, a lantern lighting the room and he would watch from outside. He couldn't see her head, it was above the window, only her body and her breasts. When he knocked on the door she would put out the lantern and all would be black and when he tried the latch he found the door barred.

She had secured the house well when first she was left alone with her small daughter. He would hammer on the door and beg and plead for her to let him in, but she never would, though he rowed in every evening for years come rain or shine like a love-sick cow, even when he saw her lumbering over on the rocks bloated with another man's child. No one ever knew who the father was. She had six more but there was never a man seen. They say it was the fishermen that she called back from the sea, even her own father, for the last child was a cretin. She had them all here in this room, with only her daughter Margaret to help her, crouching down over there by the window so she could look out to sea. They died, all six of them, she could never keep them after their third year. Though she was a healer, she couldn't save her own children, only Margaret, the child of her husband, lived.'

Hilda smells blood and the odd taint of birth; the taste of it is in the back of her throat. Suddenly the room seems cold. She wakes with a start. Light from the moon is filtering into the room Peggy is sitting in the chair next to the bed. She is knitting.

Hilda can hear Mary breathing, a low whistle at the back of her throat, and she is comforted. Maybe at last, she has turned a corner. She drifts back into sleep.

Mary is a child again, skipping,

Mary, Mary quite contrary
How does your garden grow?

Skipping down through the meadow with the stream, and the wooden bridge and she has hold of the hand of another girl. Hilda is filled with joy thinking it is her, but the girl turns and she sees it is Margaret Pascoe and her insides twist with loneliness. At the wall, Margaret passes through the gate leaving Mary on the riverbank picking the first pale yellow primroses. Hilda sees Margaret's pace slow, as she nears the house. She has become an old woman: it is Peggy. She enters the bedroom and takes Hilda's hand, leads her downstairs and across the road, and through the gate to sit with her sister on the riverbank. They are both children again. They make daisy chains out of the first primroses.

'Come, Hilda.' Peggy shakes her gently. 'Sit in my chair and hold your sister's hand.'

Hilda wakes, bewildered, 'Where are you going?'

'Mary is not much longer for this world. Come sit with her.'

At first light, Mary's breath stills. Hilda is not afraid. Her whole body is enveloped in a beautiful sadness, a sadness that fills her with love for her sister. Mary's hand is growing cold.

Peggy touches her on the shoulder. 'Thank you for letting her go.' The warmth of Peggy's hand seeps through Hilda's clothes. She shuts her eyes. She can hear the stream trickling. No it can't be. She makes to stand.

'Stay,' Peggy says.

Hilda looks up. There is something different about Peggy. Overnight her face has developed a downy softness. 'I'll go and make us a cup of tea.' She bends to smooth Mary's hair; gently kisses her on the cheek. 'She looks so at peace, so lovely; like a young girl again.'

'With silver bells and cockle shells
And pretty maids all in a row.'

They recite together.

In the room there is a strong smell of salt fish. Hilda goes over to the window and opens the sash. The tide is going out, gently scuttering the pebbles.

Singing to the men far out to sea.

The Jewel of Trabzon

We watch the women from our balcony.

'Peasants,' Zeynip spits, 'Peasants.'

'I thought you said they were from Trabzon.'

She bridles. 'Yes, they are, but they're new money, gun runners. Look at them, how they behave.'

I lean on the balcony rail and, shading my eyes from the dazzling sun, continue to watch the two women who are standing waist deep in the sea; their eyes trawling the water. They wear long flowery dresses, and headscarves fringed with flimsy ducats. The ducats hang down into their faces, casting disc-like shadows over their pale skin.

'Zeynip,' I enquire into the room, 'Why don't they put on their swimming costumes?'

'Peasants,' she spits again. 'Peasants.' She comes onto the balcony. 'Look at them, such stupid people.'

'Are they very rich?' I ask. 'They don't look it.'

'How do you think they can afford to buy a holiday home here? They are incredibly rich. Orhan says that the ring the husband threw in the sea last night was worth millions.'

The man on the balcony of the adjacent building shouts down to the women in the sea. They splash out of the water and, shading their eyes, look up at the balcony. They are women of a similar age and size; stocky in build with pale podgy faces. The one the man talks to has a

63

tooth missing at the front. Her dress clings to her body, showing large breasts with erect nipples and the beginnings of a swelling belly.

'If he is so rich,' I ask Zeynip, who is now sitting in the shadow of the balcony, 'why hasn't he got a beautiful wife?'

She pats the seat next to her. The man raises his voice, making me jump. I watch the women scurry underneath the building to climb the concrete stairs to their apartment.

'What is he saying?' I ask.

Zeynip pats the seat again, and puts a finger to her lips. 'He says that he is hungry, and if she doesn't want another beating his lunch better be on the table in half an hour.'

'Doesn't he care that people are listening?'

'No, he thinks it makes him look strong, letting people know that he can control his wife. She is a peasant woman from his village, probably a cousin. Men like that see beauty as trouble. Other men will look at her if she has beauty. And he will not want her to be educated. That also is trouble. She is little better than his dog, and so he beats her.'

'Is that what we heard last night, all that screaming?' I ask.

'The mother-in-law was meddling. That is always what causes the trouble. While the husband was away, his mother will have wanted to be in charge and probably the younger women have been disobeying her. The husband would have had to punish his wife because if he did not his

64

mother would have called him weak.'

'Why did he throw the ring in the sea?'

'He returned with it as a present for his wife. The mother-in-law said she had been looking at other men and didn't deserve it. He was so angry, he threw the ring in the sea.'

'Why would he buy a ring that was worth so much for a woman he thought a dog?'

Zeynip sighs, fed up with my many questions. 'To show his wealth of course, and also he hopes that soon she will bear him a son.'

We go inside to prepare lunch. Zeynip peels the deep purple, polished skin from three aubergines. Cupping the base of each aubergine in her hand, she removes one strip of skin revealing the white flesh underneath. Then, leaving an inch of polished skin, she repeats the pattern until the whole aubergine is striped dark purple and white.

Her hands, although small and delicate, are strong. The nails are painted a pale pink to complement her skin and the gold and diamonds she wears on her fingers.

'What shall I do, Zeynip?'

She looks up from her task. Sizing me up, she tosses her head, 'Well, the cleaning lady hasn't been yet, and the bathroom needs cleaning.'

She glances at me, 'Or you could prepare a salad.'

'I wouldn't like to do the cleaning lady out of a job, Zeynip. I'll do the salad.'

I strain the salted water off the white feta cheese, my heart pounding with anger.

'Be careful with the water,' Zeynip says. 'The water

tanker hasn't been yet.'

'Doesn't the water come through underground pipes?'

'No, we have to have the tank in the roof filled every week.'

'You would think with all this money the people along here could organise a proper supply.'

'You are cutting the pieces too big. Orhan likes his salad bits cut small.'

Lunch is the salad that I have helped make and the small, bony, battered fish, caught by the men that morning. The aubergines are for the evening meal. They lie soaking in salt water.

After lunch, the men and the children return to the boat and the sea. Zeynip and I make our way down the crumbling concrete steps to the beach. It is three o'clock in the afternoon and the sun is still high in the sky. The sand is hot beneath our feet. We spread our towels and lie down.

Zeynip's body is sleek and tawny. Mine is blobby and white. I take care to leave my sarong casually draped over the worst bits. While Zeynip sunbathes, I shade my eyes and look down the beach.

Two women walking by the shore stare at me. When I stare back they do not lower their eyes but simply meet my gaze with the unabashed curiosity of children. I stick out my tongue. There is a flicker. They scurry off. I chuckle. Zeynip sits up.

'What is it?'

'I stuck my tongue out at those two women over there.' I point down the beach.

She shades her eyes and looks. 'Ey, ey, ey, you shouldn't have done that. It is the family of Osman Bey. He is a very important man; a very rich man. Orhan respects him very much.'

'Never mind, you can say I am a crazy foreigner. A *gavur,* an eater of cheese.'

Zeynip returns to her sun worshipping. I lie down next to her and think, I too could be that colour. But after half an hour I give up. Wrapping my sarong carefully around me, I saunter down to the water's edge. The two peasant women from this morning have returned to the sea, searching again for the lost ring. They glance up to the balcony and, seeing no one, stop their task to stare at me. Their stare is somehow different from the other women's. It holds no malice. Like two sheep, they stare intently. I smile and am rewarded by two childlike grins.

'Merhaba!' I call. They wave back. Zeynip sits up, and seeing the peasant women scowls, and returns to her slumbers.

I walk along the beach towards the women. They come to the water's edge. The sand is damp and cool on the hot soles of my feet. Something sharp jabs my foot and I bend down to examine the sand. Pointing upwards out of the sand is a beautifully polished shell dappled like a leopards' skin. I dig it out with my fingers and rinse it carefully under the water. I turn it over. Nestling in the cusp of the shell is a huge ruby ring, clustered with diamonds. For one fleeting second I think to close my

67

fingers.

What difference would it make to these stupid women and the even more stupid man if the ring were lost? I look up. Both women are watching me intently, a look of animal cunning on their faces. They are suspicious; what I am rinsing at the water's edge?

'*Gel*!' I shout, 'Come'.

They come splashing through the water towards me. I open my hands and there, glistening in my cupped palm are the mottled browns of the shell. Their faces fall until, laughing, I turn the shell over to show the ring wedged in the cusp. The wife looks at me and hesitates. I tug the ring out from the crevice of the shell and taking her rough hand, place the ring in her palm.

'*Mashallah! Mashallah*!' She murmurs, looking in wonder at the ring.

Suddenly she grabs my hand and bows to kiss it and then, not satisfied with that, she kisses me roughly on both cheeks. I turn towards Zeynip, who with all the commotion is now sitting up.

'What is she saying?'

'She is saying that the *gavur* woman has brought her luck.'

I smile at the happy, guileless face. Her husband shouts from the balcony and she hurries up the beach and into the darkness of the building, followed closely by her sister.

Zeynip gets up and shakes her towel. 'Bah! Peasants!' she grumbles.

We return upstairs to the cool darkness of the flat.

68

I'm still elated from my find and feel the need to do something. 'Is there enough water for a shower, Zeynip?'

'No. I am sorry. You should have gone in the sea.'

I watch her as she prepares tea. Water in the bottom kettle with dry, unwashed tea leaves in the top kettle. When the water has boiled she will fill the top kettle, wetting the already steamed tea.

'It was a huge ring,' I say.

'Umph! Women like that don't know what to do with jewellery. You should have kept it.'

'Should I?'

'Umph!'

On a tray, we arrange small clinking glasses and white melamine saucers. Into each glass I put a tiny teaspoon, listening each time for the clink. I carry the tray through to the balcony. The men are pulling the boat out of the water and up onto the beach. The children are dancing giddily around the men. Zeynip shouts at them sternly, or so I think, but they just look up, wave, and continue their ritual dance.

The husband of the peasant woman comes out from underneath his apartment and walks up to Orhan. They shake hands and kiss on both cheeks and then the peasant man bends his head and kisses Orhan's hand. Zeynip gives a little satisfied grunt and turns to fetch the tea. I watch as the men, unsmiling, talk, then part as stiff as soldiers; a silent nod their only salute. Zeynip pours us all tea, including the children. First, a little strong black liquid from the top kettle, topped up by hot water from the bottom kettle. We all plop a sugar lump into our tea, the children two. The sound of the spoons on the tea glasses as we stir our tea is like a gentle wind chime and makes the children laugh.

'Clink, clink!' they mimic.

'What did he want?' Zeynip asks, nodding her head in the direction of next door.

'You women are invited for tea tomorrow afternoon.'

He looks at me and laughs, 'He says that the *gavur* has brought them luck.'

Drinking the last of his tea, Orhan runs his hand through his hair and stretches. 'I think I will go for a shower.'

I look at Zeynip. She averts her eyes.

The evening meal is to be *Imam Bayildi,* 'the priest has fainted'. Aubergines stuffed with spiced mince, accompanied by soup and rice and stuffed vine leaves. I have the job of peeling and chopping the onions. Zeynip is carefully parcelling the rice and nuts into individual vine leaves.

'Don't you ever get fed up, spending all your time cooking?'

Zeynip shrugs. 'No. Why should I? It is my duty.'

'Have you no hobbies?'

She points to a small disc on the wall, the size of a small saucer. It is a frieze of a cottage, like the Gingerbread house in *Hansel and Gretel*. It is painted in bright oranges and yellows.

'Have you made this?' I say, unhooking it from the wall to get a closer look.

'Yes. I go to a modelling class.'

'It is very beautiful.'

Zeynip smiles. We hear shouting from the bathroom next door. Zeynip hurries off and returns for the bottle of fresh water. 'The water has run out and Orhan is covered in soap.'

I try not to laugh. Zeynip looks at me.

'These onions are very strong,' I say.

Two hours later, the ritual of the meal over, Zeynip and I sit in the quiet of the evening. The men have gone to find water. The children murmur from their bedroom. I would have liked to go with the men but was not invited. Zeynip switches on the black and white television. I recognise the film but not the voices. It is *Cat on a Hot Tin Roof*, dubbed. We do not have to listen to the shrieks of Elizabeth Taylor, but to the sultry voice of a stranger. I go out onto the balcony. The beach is quiet now, the sea, still. The moon sits low on the horizon. How did I come to this strange and wonderful land?

Why do I feel trapped?

The next day, lunch dispensed with, the smell of oil hanging heavy in the air, Zeynip and I sit sleepily on the balcony, enjoying the quiet.

I ask, 'When do we go next door?'

'We will have to wait until after the third prayer call, *al asr*. The old lady has to pray.'

'Do we have to go?'

'Yes. They would be very insulted if we did not go, and Orhan would be very angry.'

'Why doesn't he go, then?'

'He says it is "woman's business".'

I must have slumbered because I am awoken by a jingling sound. Zeynip is standing before me, decked out in all her wealth, gold dripping from her neck and wrists and she has on yet another ring, a huge emerald encrusted with diamonds. Her hair has been swept back and in her ears, huge diamonds sparkle. She is wearing a pale pink tailored dress and pale pink sling-back shoes in fine, soft, pink leather.

'Wow, Zeynip. Where are you going?'

'Next door, of course.'

'Do I have to get dressed up?'

Zeynip shrugs, 'It's up to you.'

The wife answers the door. She is still wearing a headscarf, but now it is tied around her head and knotted at the top, Gypsy fashion. Her dress is very similar to the one she had on yesterday, but is obviously newer. She greets us warmly, kissing us on both cheeks, ignoring Zeynip's carefully powdered cheek. We are taken through to the lounge. The curtains are drawn, protecting the room and its occupants from the afternoon sun. A huge, glistening chandelier hung with hundreds of tiny crystals lights the room. Seated in an enormous armchair is an old lady. She is dressed entirely in black, including a headscarf she wears low over her leathery face. Zeynip crosses the room to where the old lady sits. The old lady proffers her hand. Zeynip raises it to her lips and from there to her forehead. I follow suit and the old lady cackles in surprise. She turns to talk to Zeynip. They think I don't understand. They are saying what they always say:

'She is not ugly, is she?'

The sister enters the room carrying a tray of tea glasses. She puts it down on the coffee table and comes to greet Zeynip and myself.

We are fed little pastries filled with nuts and smothered in syrup so sickly I want to gag. They watch my face with anticipation.

I sip at my tea, 'Very beautiful,' I say holding up the pastry. '*Çok güzel.*'

The wife goes to the kitchen and returns with more. My refusal is ignored.

Nesame, as we learn the wife is called, comes and sits next to me. She takes my hand and smiles happily into my face. I cannot understand what she is saying and turn to Zeynip.

'She says that you are a very good friend to her and have brought her much luck.'

I take Nesame's hand. She is wearing the ring from the sea. It sits strangely on her large hand.

'What does she say, Zeynip?'

'Oh, nothing important.'

But I understand what Nesame is saying. 'This ring has been in my husband's family for many generations.'

I look at Zeynip and smile. She tosses her head and looks away. Zeynip is a newcomer; she is not of old stock. She met her husband while at university. Orhan's family disapproved of his choice, said she was not from a good family and would only bring trouble.

There is a knock at the door. Nesame runs to answer

it. She guides in two women, one portly and middle-aged, the other a teenage girl in her first bloom. They are both dressed in a similar fashion to Zeynip, decked in expensive jewellery and wearing designer frocks and shoes.

They greet us all, and we return the greetings in the traditional manner. When we are seated again, they turn to smile and stare at me.

The portly woman, Fatma, addresses Zeynip, 'She is not ugly, is she?'

'What are you saying?' I ask Zeynip.

'I am asking her to forgive your strange manners.'

'What do you mean?'

'These are the women you stuck your tongue out at yesterday.'

I blush and the women laugh. Nesame slaps me on the back and laughs into my face. I laugh back, enjoying her childlike frivolity.

The heat of the afternoon lulls us. The old woman dozes, unconsciously fondling the prayer beads in her lap. The teenage girl, Sibyl, comes to sit next to me while Zeynip talks to her mother. Nesame sits at our feet and smiles up at us. She has removed her headscarf revealing her poor flattened hair.

'Do you like our country then?' asks Sibyl, in perfect English.

Her mother says something and they laugh.

'My mother says, if you like the men, you have to like the country.'

Sibyl strokes Nesame's hair. 'We are cousins, you know.'

74

'I don't understand,' I say, 'Zeynip said...'

'I said you were all from Trabzon,' Zeynip butts in.

'You are not, though, Zeynip, are you?' The portly woman smiles. Zeynip flushes bright red, though whether through embarrassment or anger I am not sure.

'Zeynip is an educated woman, though,' I say, 'It doesn't matter where she comes from.'

The portly woman smiles graciously.

'I am going to go to university in a month's time,' Sibyl says proudly, 'I am going to become a civil engineer.'

'Or become a housewife like the rest of us,' Zeynip says, cynically.

'Are you a housewife?' Sibyl asks, turning to me.

'No.'

'I'll be like you, then.' She smiles.

As we are leaving, Nesame presents me with a soft package.

'She wants you to remember her,' Zeynip translates.

I open the package. It is a white tablecloth, exquisitely embroidered in rich coloured threads.

'Have you made this?' I gesture.

Nesame shakes her head.

'That means she has,' says Zeynip.

That evening I pack my bag. Zeynip unhooks from the wall the picture frieze of the cottage that she has so lovingly moulded.

'For you. Maybe you will remember me, too.'

A Burning Fire

The headlights of his brother's car light up the sign momentarily as they speed along the country road in the half light; an old piece of wood painted in jagged black letters, an arrow pointing down a lane part-registers in his brain - *Firewood for Sale.*

A weekend away, the first time in years as a family: mother, father and three grown-up kids. No partners, just themselves.

Don shares a bedroom with his brother: they haven't done that in years. He awakes just as it is getting light; his brother's clothes neatly folded on the chair and then his, a crumpled heap on the floor. He thinks back to when they were kids. Nothing has changed.

He hears his parents go downstairs, waits for the TV to go on, but nothing. He knows he should get up, keep them company. Waiting, slipping in and out of sleep, he hopes his sister will get up before him - he knows his brother won't - or even better, that his mother will bring them up a cup of tea as she always had; along with her gentleness, an acceptance that it was all right to start another day. When they were at home he would hear her in the kitchen, taking off the tea caddy lid, water running in the pipes, the grate of metal on metal: the kettle going on the gas.

A Burning Fire

He gets up and dresses without showering. His brother is lying on his back, breathing like Darth Vader. He rattles back the curtains. His brother doesn't stir. The tarmac road outside is black with rain.

The stairs creak as he descends. He ducks his head to avoid the beam at the bottom. They are sitting in silence in the winged chairs on either side of the fireplace, the empty grate cheerless between them.

'Thought you two would be well ensconced.' He peers out of the window. 'Shame about the rain. What would you like to do today?'

His father picks up yesterday's paper, turns to the sports page, doesn't answer.

'Aren't you making a brew?' His mother clutches her arms to her chest, 'We haven't had one yet.'

'Why not?' He hears his voice rise in pitch.

His father folds the paper in half, scores along the centre with his finger and thumb, 'Waiting for you lot. Bloody parched we are.'

It was always the same. He was the oldest, so he carried the can. His sister had these marvellous plans and then once she'd spun them out into the ether she'd sit back and watch the show. He was the one that had thought to stop at the garage on the way back from their pub meal last night to get milk and tea and bread and all the things he knew his parents would want for breakfast.

He tries not to bang things around in the kitchen. It wasn't their fault. They hadn't wanted to come in the first place, had they?

He drops three tea bags into three cups, looks around for the toaster but there isn't one. He has to use the grill on the electric cooker. He burns the first lot; he isn't used to toasting white bread. One slice for his mother, two each for him and his father. He lets the toast cool off a bit first, his mother doesn't like the butter melted in. He scoops out the marmalade – shit, it's 'thick cut'- his father only likes 'thin cut.' He picks out the thickest bits of peel and hopes his father won't notice.

He puts everything on a tray and carries it through with a flourish, like he'd seen waiters do in restaurants, pushing the door open with his bum. He's decided to make the best of this weekend; the other two can go hang, he's going to make his parents happy, give them something to talk about when they go in The Club.

His father spots it straight away, 'You know I don't like thick cut.'

He wants to tell him to shut up, to stop being such a baby.

His mother does it for him. 'Have you heard yourself? You're like a bloody bairn.'

His father leaves his plate on the coffee table, picks up his tea, 'There's no sugar in me tea, even.'

His mother smiles up at him apologetically, takes a sip of hers, 'Nor mine, love.'

He isn't used to putting sugar in anyone's tea. He gets up, fetches the bag and a teaspoon from the kitchen. He knows he should put the sugar in a bowl but he doesn't, tears open the top of the bag instead and watches as the grains of sugar spread over the French polish of the coffee table. He spoons three sugars into his father's tea, one into his mother's, and stirs them both. 'There!'

His mother smiles again, 'Thank you, love.'

He takes a bite of his toast. White bread. He loves the synthetic nothingness of it, wonders why he eats brown.

His father watches him, his toast cooling on his plate.

'Dad, if I could drive, I'd go and get you some thin cut.'

'Whose idea was it to stay out here in the middle of bloody nowhere anyway?'

'All right Dad, what would you like to do today?' He cringes at the patronising tone of his voice. He sounds just like his sister.

'There's nothing to do.' His father plonks his cup back down on the table.

He casts around in his mind and realises his father is right. There was nothing to do. His mother can't walk far and it's raining. They could go for another pub meal, but then what would they do tonight? He'd bought some pies at the garage. They could warm those for lunch.

'She,' he looks up to the ceiling, 'will probably want to play Scrabble or something when she gets up.'

His father snorts, 'She... can please her bloody self.'

His mother holds her cup to her cheek. 'Never mind love, there's not that much of the day left anyway.'

'We could play pontoon. I wonder if there's a pack of cards here. I always used to win at that.' He rubs his hands together.

His father picks up his tea again, 'I'll still need me paper.'

He notes that his own paper is still unread from last night, 'Well, when his lordship deigns to gets up, I'm sure he'll take you for one.'

At 11.30, his brother and sister get up, fight over who is going in the bathroom first. His brother loses, takes his father to the garage for a paper. Don takes a shower after his sister, lets her make mother another cup of tea.

Dressing in the bedroom, he sees the black BMW draw up, sees them get out laughing. His brother always was easier with Dad, they seemed to speak the same language.

Downstairs someone has turned on the TV. He knows it will have been his brother. He loathes it. Just as he was beginning to open up possibilities, his brother pulls it all back to how he thinks it should be.

'What shall we do this aft then?' Again, he sounds like his sister.

'Me and Dad are going to watch footie.' He notices his brother has bought a few cans of beer.

'And the rest of us are going to do what? Mother, would you like to go out somewhere? Go into Buxton, have a look round the shops?'

She shrugs, 'Not bothered, really.'

He looks to his sister.

'Let's just stay in like a family… talk about things.'

'What, with the bloody telly on?'

A Burning Fire

He goes into the kitchen, gets out the pies, looks for the microwave. There isn't one. He leaves the pies in their foil trays and puts them in the oven. He wishes he hadn't come. It all feels so wrong, so awkward, like actors on a stage. His parents deserve better than this. He so wishes he could be a boy again, just for this weekend, remembering how good, how safe it had felt back then. He grieved for those times, wished he didn't feel such terrible guilt at having grown apart. He'd tried so hard not to.

The football starts. He likes football. Enjoys watching it, but not today.

'I think I'll go and fetch some firewood, does anyone else want to come? We could have a fire, make it cosy.'

His father looks up from his paper, 'Why can't you just sit like the rest of us? You always have to be doing. If they'd wanted us to have a fire they'd have bloody left us some wood. I don't want a fire.'

Looking back, Don noted that he'd heard that edginess, that urgency in his father's voice. His last statement had been a plea, not a request. He'd ignored it, gone out into the rain, out into the light slipping into late afternoon in late winter, walked back along the road, took the lane, followed the arrow, the sign saying, *Firewood for sale* One mile, two miles, an arrow pointing down a road should mean half a mile, max.

Life was strange, things had been the same for years. They had all been lulled by the gentle monotony of it but, this year... wham! From out of nowhere it had all changed. Mum first, with her health scare. All her life she'd looked after them and then suddenly she needed their help. She'd given up cigarettes, taken time off work, then said she missed her friends. He worried about her. What did they mean by a health scare anyway? While he was teaching, this picture of her would come suddenly into his head; their living room, the autumn leaves carpet, the TV always on in the corner, an empty ashtray. She'd refused to throw out the ashtrays, said it would be like throwing out the clothes of a dead child.

Then his father, who one day had been getting up at half six, making his own snap and then off to work for nine hours... the next, well, he'd still got up at half six, turned on the TV...

'Redundant' was the word they'd used. He had thought at the time what a heavy-sounding word it was.

He had hoped that his father would look after Mum , share more of their time together, but no, he'd curled up in his own corner, wanted someone to look after him. Depression, the doctor called it. His mother hadn't been sympathetic, said he always did want all the attention and men were just big babies.

An hour later, just as he is thinking of turning back, he sees the firewood sheltered from the rain under a corrugated lean-to, the logs stacked as tight as a new pack of cigarettes.

They are sold by the sack, kept round the back of the lean-to, lumpy, and damp from the rain. He thinks of asking for a lift back in the red pick-up with the big tyres that stands in the yard, but the words stay in his throat. For the first half-mile the sack isn't heavy, but then the sharpness of the split wood begins to dig into his back and increase in heaviness with every passing mile. He thinks about putting the sack down and taking out some of the logs, or ringing his brother, ask him to come and pick him up. He thinks of them all clustered round the TV, probably with a cup of tea and a biscuit, the custard creams he'd got for his father at the garage last night. His mother would be holding the words, making comments about what was on the screen. The cottage should have bloody well provided the wood for the rent it had cost them. He would put that in the visitors book. *No wood!* Cheerless bloody rip-off.

It is pitch black by the time he gets back. They've switched on a light, a table lamp. It looks quite cosy through the window, his mother is sitting on the sofa with her feet under her. He thinks how differently he might have felt if he'd come here with his lover, how they could have curled up on the hearthrug in front of a fire and listened to the night outside.

His sister asks if he would like a cup of tea. He says no, I want to get the fire lit first.

'I don't want you to light the fire,' his father says, his voice all stretched out like an elastic band. He should have registered it.

'I've just walked miles in the rain and cold and dark to get this wood. We're having a fire… end of.'

His sister puts on her bouncy voice, 'It'll be nice, more cheerful. Let our Don light the fire.'

'Please thi' bloody self. Never did take any notice of

me anyway.'

His mother tucks in like a bird, doesn't speak.

He uses his unread *Guardian* to light the fire. He doesn't use his father's paper, even though he's read it. He tears a page in half, rolls it in a strip and then ties it in a half bow like he remembers from Scouts. He places the half bows in the grate, puts some small pieces of wood on top and strikes a match. The flame begins to take, tentatively at first, and then it leaps into life. He places more wood on until, confident that it will take, he sits back on his heels. 'There, isn't that grand?'

Suddenly a sound fills the room; a long low wail like an animal caught in a snare. He turns, tries to stand, sees his father stumble and lurch from the room, his whole body shaking uncontrollably. He wants to move but the shock has transfixed him. He looks at his sister and she is the same, her mouth half open, even his brother has been disturbed enough to glance away from the TV. On his mother's face there is a just a faint trace of irritation.

All three of them stand on the landing, listening through the locked bedroom door for any sounds, but nothing.

'Dad, let us in,' his sister pleads.

Ten minutes, twenty minutes they wait, occasionally hearing a faint, indistinguishable sound like a suppressed yelp.

His sister bangs on the door again. 'Dad, let us in please. We're worried about you.'

His brother takes her arm, 'It won't do any good, let him be for a while.'

They go back downstairs. Their mother is still sitting on the sofa, tucked in even tighter.

'Mother, what's wrong with him? Has this happened before?' he asks.

'You shouldn't have lit that fire.'

'Has he done it before?'

She shakes her head, 'He was all right 'til you lit that fire.'

His brother makes a cup of tea. They sit looking at each other. The news comes on the TV. His eyes are drawn to the newsreader.

'Why don't you go up?' his sister asks. He pulls his eyes away from the TV to find she is addressing his mother. 'He might let you in.'

'You three wanted this weekend. You sort it.'

His sister raises her eyes to the ceiling. He follows suit, straining for any sound, any movement through the floorboards.

'Poor Dad,' his sister says. 'We could go up one by one, talk to him. He'll be all right if we just talk to him.'

'What about?' his brother asks. 'The door's locked, anyway.'

'Well… you can talk to him about football, he'll like that, and I'll talk to him about,' she pauses, 'holidays we used to have, like that one when we went to Cornwall, that was good.'

'And me?' he asks.

'You, you just talk to him. You'll know what to say.'

'For Christ's sake, the man's just lost his bloody

85

job. What am I going to say to him?'

Why did they always think he could sort everything?

' Mum ?' he appeals.

She tucks in tighter still, like an origami bird, glues her eyes to the television and he sees a fear in her eyes that he has never seen before. This is all his fault. As usual he had tried to paper over the cracks but what he'd actually done was crack everything wide open. The fire is fading. He wants to kick the logs, break them, see them crumble like this family's façade.

He tries the black metal latch. 'Dad? Let us in.' There is a pleading edge to his voice, 'We're all worried about you downstairs and, you know the doc said, Mum isn't to get stressed.'

He hears the pad of slippers across the floor, the lifting of the chain, the feet padding back. He holds his breath, then tries the door. It opens. His father is in darkness, sitting hunched over on the edge of the bed. An orange street lamp partly lights the room. He sits down next to his father; eldest son, close but not touching. Like his father, he leans on his elbows in silence. He knows they will be listening downstairs.

'I'm sorry, Dad.'

After five minutes, 'What for, son?'

'For lighting the fire. I should have listened to you.'

His father doesn't reply.

Five minutes, ten minutes... he watches the rain falling around the streetlight. A streetlight out in the country. They should have stayed at home, stayed where their father was king of his own castle.

He hears his father whisper, listens hard to catch the words.

'All wasted... all those years a foundry man, shovelling coke to keep the furnace going... and for what? On the scrap heap. Sixty-three... and on the bloody scrap heap.'

'You have your freedom now,' he whispers back, 'That's what you always wanted.'

'Nay, lad. They took that too. You try setting a tamed fox free. It'd be kinder to knock it on the head.'

'Dad, that's not true.'

'You'd know would you? Spent the last forty-odd years doing a job you hated, have you? Had your soul and your strength leached out of you, have you? Just a dried-up old biscuit is all I am now.'

He watches the rain fall around the street lamp, watches how the rain turns to orange beads of light and then drops into darkness.

'Glad of that, though...'

'What, Dad?'

'That you three have all got good lives. I'm glad of that.'

'But Dad, you can have a good life now, you and Mum can spend time together.'

He hears a choking sound, he turns, his father is clutching at his throat, trying to hold back the sound.

It comes out as a long soft moan.

'Dad, what is it?' He can feel tears rising in his throat. 'What is it?'

A Burning Fire

'Your mother says she's going to leave me.'

'What?'

'You heard.'

'She doesn't mean it.'

'And you'd know would you? His father puts his hand up to Don's cheek, wipes away a tear.

He can't imagine it: returning to the sanctuary of his parents' home and his mother not being there.

'She doesn't mean it, Dad. You know Mum , she couldn't cope without you.'

His father gets up, goes over to the window. 'It's like staring into a gaping hole, like when we used to let the furnaces go out in the summer so they could repair the bricks inside, like you're staring into nothing.'

'It's just Mum being Mum .'

His father turns, looks out of the window, 'Leave me, son. Let me have a bit of peace.'

'Dad!'

'I've already lost me dignity once, now leave me be.'

He tries to stop his brother following him up, but only manages to stay him for half an hour. When his brother comes down his sister goes up armed with tea and biscuits.

They wait downstairs in silence, he sits on the sofa next to his mother, takes her hand. It is like a child's in his man's hand. She closes her eyes, smiles.

His sister brings their father back down, resting on her arm. He thinks how frail he looks. His mother still has her eyes closed. His father looks wistful, sad. He sits down in his chair next to the table lamp. The room is quiet except for the game show on TV. His sister sits down on the arm of her father's chair, 'Are you okay, Dad?'

'I would be,' he says, 'but you've let the bloody fire go out.'

Anna Kare-nina

A dark blue, leather bound book juts from a wound of split pomegranate flesh where the metal wheels of the train have met the metal track. A rag doll woman; jersey dress of pale cream clinging to the curve of her breast, the indent of her waist, the hem lifted by the back draught showing satin knickers, a deep, russet red like the blood on her dress. A suspender strap stretches over dimpled white flesh, tugs at a black stocking. One black patent shoe; the other is missing. Dressed for an event, around her neck are two unbroken strings of pearls; no prizes for the station jackdaws.

I want to know the name of her book.

Every weekday morning I saw her, stale and biscuit-like; hair dyed to straw, face downy with powder, clothes tired from the wash, an old-fashioned raincoat, legs and shoes grey-dust weary. Only her handbag was smart, high class, designer label. Now it is missing.

As I clattered down to catch the incoming train it became a game to see whether she would be standing at the bottom of the steps. We took to smiling shyly and later, a nod. Sometimes we would sit opposite each other on the train and get out our books: hers an old fashioned hard back with a plain cover; a name I could never read. Mine always the same book - *The Diary of Bridget Jones* -

I could never read further than the first page, the language was too difficult. She would glance at me when she thought I wasn't looking, checking to see if it was still the same book. She must have wondered at the slow speed of my reading.

Over time she began to bother me. I saw in her my reflection, working all day in a dark office, surrounded by grey filing cabinets, piles of old receipts balanced on top, gathering dust, adding rows of figures, each day merging into another, each night going back to an empty flat. I did not want to become her, seeking out the distant comfort of strangers on trains.

In the mornings I began to look down at the white lines along the edges of the stone steps, taking my time, waiting until the carriage filled before getting out my book. Twenty minutes later I would see her getting out at the stop before mine, Elephant and Castle.

The ambulance men arrive, full of siren importance. Station staff in their pale-green uniforms force us back. I push through them, crouch at the edge of the platform.

'I knew her,' I say, but only loud enough for the man who is nearest to me on the track to hear. He picks up the book and turns. He looks very young. I get out my red plastic bag, quickly scoop the foil package of my sandwiches from the bottom, stuff them in my pocket and open the bag wide for him. He moves towards me, his step is uncertain; he looks into my face and then not knowing what else to do, drops the book into the red plastic bag.

'What was her name?'

I look down into the bag, along the spine of the book.

'Anna, Anna Kare-nina,' I try to say it in my best English.

'Was she foreign?'

'Yes, Polish. I think.'

They manage to keep her body together. With care, they turn her head and make a cup shape with their hands, cradling her straw-like hair. The young ambulance man is sick between the tracks. Still wiping his mouth with the back of his hand, he is sent to look up and down the line for her other shoe, her bag. He looks at me. I shake my head.

Before climbing to safety they place the stretcher, covered in a crimson red blanket, on the edge of the platform. The stretcher pole touches the white painted line. The wires whir, the points click and in the distance I can hear the waiting train and then the sound of the siren fills my head.

I know where the drug addicts go to strip handbags and wallets of cash. Behind the ladies toilet block, amongst the thrown away condoms, I find it. A slim, hard, tortoiseshell bag with a gold snap and chain, the one she always wore on Fridays. I hide it in the red plastic bag and go with the policeman. I do not tell him my real name. I tell them her name is Miss Anna Kare-nina, it suits her. I wonder why I have never named her before. I tell the policeman that I have known her years, a single woman with no relatives. They ask me if I will go to the mortuary to identify her body. I say I will, the next day.

Anna Kare-nina

My flat is above the off-licence on the main road, water dripping off black metal stairs, a door, dark blue, tarnished brass knocker, round leaded window. I put the key in the lock, pull it out a fraction, turn it slowly, listen for the click, watch as the door swings open.

I see it as if for the first time. A blue-patterned, old-fashioned carpet, faded grey wallpaper, a bed unmade, a pink candlewick bedspread, a smell of cheap talc. On my bedside table a tarnished silver frame holding a black and white photo of a man with small teeth and a weak chin. A plate and knife in the sink. Red jam. A diary. Blank page after blank page, then today, '*Andrew*'.

I get ready: run water into the bath, pour oil of aloe vera under the tap to make my skin soft. Put on my red satin knickers, the ones he loves, the ones that I don't have to take off. Clean sheets. Smoked salmon. A bottle of sweet white wine. I fill a vase with water and lemonade, for the flowers that he will bring me.

I run the tortoiseshell handbag under the tap, wash off the blood, wipe it dry with paper towels, spill the contents out onto the table:

A lipstick, blood red.

A compact.

A packet of Polo mints, unopened.

Two Yale keys.

A brass key, a tag - the numbers – 101.

A crumpled slip of paper, an address: 30C Bagshaw Drive.

I leave the book in the red bag; place it on the draining board, wait for Andrew. He doesn't come.

I twist the keys in my pocket. 30C Bagshaw Drive. I learn the address by heart, catch the train to Elephant and Castle, take a left after the petrol station, the third house on the right. A house with a pointed gable, green paint flaking off carved wood. I ring the doorbell and wait. I try the key with the 101 tag on, it doesn't work. I try the first key on the ring with two keys on. It doesn't work. I try the next key, push the door slowly open. All the rooms have locks, I knock lightly, wait and then try the second key on the ring. Her room is on the second floor, it is pink and lilac, it smells of old men. On the bed is a pink nylon-quilted counterpane. There are no photographs, no documents, no clothes, no handbags, nothing of Anna. The bathroom is down the hall.

I start catching a later train. Stop reading my book, start watching people, seeing what papers or books they read. I have to stand, hold onto the rail by the door, look down at all the other outstretched arms holding on beneath mine, with watches telling nearly the same time. Sturdy shoes, badly worn brogues cracked like old baseball gloves, plump feet pushed into red stilettos. Yellow light splashing on graffiti walls. A man bouncing up the station steps in front of me showing black socks, a hole in each heel. I miss the biscuit woman. I should have been kinder to her.

I was there at Anna's burial. They cut the iron hard ground with steel, slicing bulbs. I was the only mourner, not like at my mother's funeral where I had to push through all the legs to see the grave. The Madame had bought me new shoes, white ankle socks and a grey coat with a velvet collar. Afterwards, two women took me to the children's home, smiled their broken teeth at me, smudged their orange lipstick on my cheek; the smell of them, cheap perfume and sweat, like my mother, except my mother had another scent too, in the hollow under her chin.

They told me that my father would come for me.

I spent my savings on a woman I'd never spoken to. A headstone of plain slate, and the words, *Anna Karenina* written in gold letters. No birth date, no death date, just her name. After the burial I went for coffee and a cream cake on the high street, fingered the Yale keys in my pocket, the door key, all three now on the same ring.

I had taken the police to the room at 30C Bagshaw Drive. They drove me there in a police car. I was afraid. They told me the landlord was a Mr Brodski, untraceable. Anna, they said, had thrown away all her belongings on purpose but I couldn't help wondering about the key in my pocket with the tag 101.

I went home and took her book out of the red plastic bag, used a damp cloth to wipe the cover. The cloth was smeared a pale rust red, the gold leaf edge spattered the colour of her blood. The pages that would open were crisp as bank notes, I counted the date stamps. Always the book was borrowed in winter. Anna Kare-nina what a lovely name.

I dream at night of Anna. I am standing at the bottom of the stone steps and she is coming down, slowly, with precision, holding onto the handrail. The draught lifts the hem of her cream dress. I catch a glimpse of the flesh above her stockings.

I smile, 'You look different today.'

Her voice is stretched out, lazy. 'You notice. Thank you. They like my dress you know.'

'Who like your dress?' I have taken her accent.

'Punters,' I think you say.

I frown. 'Punters?'

'So horny in the morning they are.' She laughs a shrill cheap laugh. It wakes me up. I turn on the light. Pick up the photo of the man with the weak chin. He has small teeth. 'Punters,' I stretch out the word. My voice sounds different, I am different.

A month passes. I fill a vase with lemonade and water, place it on the windowsill. Go to the delicatessen and buy smoked salmon and a sweet white wine. I want halva, I cannot find it. I have to ask for it, talk to the man behind the counter for the first time. He is puzzled and looks into my face, trying to recognise my accent.

He asks me a question in my own language. I do not reply.

I put on red silk knickers, the matching bra, and wait. Andrew is very late. I want to tell him about Anna but he is in a hurry. He makes me stand at the sink. He does not remove my knickers.

I awake in the morning. The sun is shining through the water in the glass vase. I dress and go down to the Saturday market to buy flowers. I purchase two small bunches of yellow flowers, still in bud. The man behind the stall tells me they are called daffodils. I say the word slowly, it is a nice word. I climb the stone steps to the library; I have never entered a library before. I ask a woman sitting behind a desk, 'Have you got a book called Anna Kare-nina?'

'Anna Karenina,' she corrects me, then smiles a crooked tooth smile. 'Think she died on a railway track a while back.'

I wonder how she knows. 'Was it in the paper?' I ask.

She taps her keyboard, clucks her teeth, 'Our copy should have been returned weeks ago, people are very bad you know.' She swivels the screen to show me. November, I read. A number, a name, Karen Lewenski. An address in very small letters. I can only read the numbers 101.

I go to the cemetery. Small white flowers, the first milk teeth of spring, poke through the grass. I crouch down and place the daffodils on her grave. Next time I will bring a vase. I tell her that her flowers are called daffodils. I tell her it is a nice word.

More blank diary pages and two months pass. I visit the cemetery every week. I take flowers every month. I tell Anna how I am catching the later train now, and that how behind the ladies toilet block I found a handbag with two hundred pounds hidden in the lining.

When the sun is hot I walk in the shade of the chestnut trees down to the Saturday market. I buy flowers. The man behind the stall tells me their name. Sweet peas, locally grown, he says. They have the scent of old-fashioned about them, the scent of my mother.

It is the month after this that Andrew comes. I am glad to see him. He says I look better with my hair dyed yellow; younger, different. We have sex. He makes me stand out on the gantry, the light is mauve. I watch as the streetlights flicker on one by one. See his hands grasping the metal rail, his gold ring. I remember when he used to take me to expensive hotels and buy me jewellery.

I write in my diary after he leaves; *Andrew came to see me today.*

Again I dream of Anna, a younger Anna. She is sitting on a beach, her skirt pulled up above her knees. Next to her sits a young man. He is bending his head trying to look up into her face,

'Please Anna, you have to go, it will be our future.'

'No.'

'We can marry when you return.'

'But I don't speak the language.'

'They are a good family. Well behaved children.'

'Come with me then.' She digs her toes into the sand.

'I can't, I will stay here, build our future.' He stands, hauls her to her feet, drags her towards the sea.

I feel the water, warm, lapping my feet. It wakes me.

A man has positioned a tall ladder against the gable. He is scraping away at loose green paint. He glances around as I lift the metal catch on the gate. I am of no importance. He continues with his work. The path is untidy with the first leaves of autumn. I stand in the porch and take the keys out of my pocket. I look at them wondering whether to ring the doorbell first.

I hear the sound of someone coming down the stairs. The man outside is moving his ladder.

A man, small, dark and plump, has opened the door. 'Ha. Good. You have come.'

I follow him slowly up the stairs. He hauls himself up on the stair rail, breathing heavily. He enters Anna's room.

He stares at me. 'You are very nice. Please remove your clothes.'

I stare at him.

He looks at his watch. 'I have been waiting for you one whole hour.'

I shake my head. He takes out his wallet. He counts out onto the table five notes, 'One hundred pounds is what is agreed. Yes?'

I am back there all those years ago when I first came to this country.

I nod, 'Yes, it is correct.' My voice is stretched out, lazy.

I wish I had worn my silk knickers. He sits and watches as I undress; clasping his hands together; plump hands, black hair on the flat parts of his fingers.

He croons, 'Ah, so nice.'

I stand, awkward, shivering, bend to pick up my dress.

'Please don't be afraid. I only want to look, to touch. I am a man of ill health.'

He beckons me to him. His hands are soft, dry and

very gentle. He strokes the contours of my waist, the underside of my breasts, the soft skin of my inner thighs, the wet pink flesh between my legs all the while groaning softly to himself, 'So beautiful...'

It is the first time I have ever been told. The chair he is sitting on creaks under his weight. His hair is thinning on top; thin black and grey strands across a pale pink scalp. The oil in his hair is heavy with perfume.

He asks me to return the following week. 'You are so much more beautiful than her,' he tells me. 'So much sweeter. I told her last time she came not to come again if she couldn't be civil. I didn't mean it, all these weeks, months I have waited, every Friday. It was worth the wait though.' He smiles at me.

I tell him her name was Anna.

We meet every week. I leave work at three and catch the train one station down the line. I fill my diary out weekly now. I buy new underwear, put on stockings. Sometimes I just sit on his lap and he holds me like a small child.

I ask him to tell me of Anna.

'When I got too ill for sex she came instead, she wasn't a proper lady of the night you know, as she kept telling me. 'Have you done pawing me,' she'd say. She was a very cold woman, said I ought to be grateful that she came here at all, she didn't like coming here. The hooker that used to come, she liked it here, said at least it was warm. When I got ill she offered to find me someone else, said she'd got a neighbour who was looking for company and extra cash. She said I'd like her.'

I buy flowers; their heads fill the cupped palm of my hands, deep russet red, pale pink, candlewick pink, and a dark pink, edging to mauve. The flower man tells me their name but he has to write it down for me before I can say it – Chrysanthemums. I put half in my vase filled with water and lemonade.

Andrew came last night, knocked on my door, used the brass knocker. I did not let him in. I take the other half of the flowers to the cemetery. I tell Anna that I visit the plump man every week. He has taken to bringing me presents, hand-made chocolates in gold boxes, tied with red ribbons, and last week he brought me a dozen red roses. He says I am beautiful. He has asked me my name. I shall tell him on Friday.

It is my birthday. I buy a pomegranate from the greengrocers. A November birthday, it says on my birth certificate. I rummage in the boxes outside the second hand bookshop. A hardback copy of *Anna Karenina*. I open the front cover, £1, written in pencil. I shall take it with me every day to read on the train. Now I can read her story. I hope it is a good story with a happy ending.

The woodwork on the gable is bare. The frost is early; the man has left it too late to paint. I let myself in and climb the stairs two at a time. A man, wolf-like, hair pulled back into a ponytail is pacing up and down the room. I recognise him from long ago.

I am flying across the room. I crash into the chair. It breaks under my weight. He is shouting at me in my language. He pulls me to my feet. Where is the plump man? I want to ask.

'Where is she?'

I do not speak.

'I know she's been seeing an extra punter. I want my money you bitch!'

I shake my head.

He raises his hand; he has many rings on his fingers. I move my head sideways. He stops, grunts, 'No, I won't mark you.' He shakes me. I hear my teeth rattle.

'Whore.'

I do not speak. I must not speak.

'The decorator told me, you and her thought you'd been very clever didn't you?'

He looks at me, eyes part closed, a look of half recognition.

I see him now. He was the man waiting for me when I got off the boat. I was young then. I pray he will not remember.

'You think you can trick me, you whores, but then your punters go and die outside here on the footpath and the police come poking their noses around. Where is my money?' He puts his hand around my throat.

This is not real; soon I shall awake. The plump man will be holding my hand, looking up into my face, telling me how beautiful I am.

The door bell rings. I see blue light flashing on the ceiling.

The big blooms of chrysanthemums have passed. I buy the smaller heads now, the colours are deeper, richer, the red

Anna Kare-nina

darker. I do not visit Anna for many weeks. I do not know what to say. I stay in bed for a whole week.

I dream I am a child again. The black and white man with the weak chin is crouching down beside me. The sun is high in the sky. We are at the bottom of some stone steps in front of a big stone building. He tells me, in his posh voice, that it is the parliament building of our country. He asks me if I would like an ice cream. He smiles. He has small teeth. I watch as he walks away.

Later, a policeman finds me; takes me back to the children's home.

I visit Anna, take a bunch of prickly leaves with red berries, I do not ask their name. Someone has placed a jar with plastic flowers on her grave; I tell her I am sorry that I have not visited. I have been sad for the plump man. I put the plastic flowers under the hedge; place my circle of glossy leaves on her grave. On the way home I take the Yale keys for Bagshaw Drive off my key ring, drop them down a grate, put my hand in my pocket, feel the roundness of the 101 tag, the coldness of Anna's door key. I return to the library and tell them my name is Karen Lewenski, they ask me my address.

I start catching the earlier train again and, as I clatter down the steps to the platform, I imagine that the biscuit woman is standing at the bottom. She has a new handbag. It is red. I am not sure whether it is leather or not.

She speaks to me. I am startled. She asks my name.
I say it is Anna Kare-nina. She looks puzzled.

She has a new book, a hard back with a plain cover. I cannot read the name. Again I read the first line in my book. - *Happy families are all alike; every unhappy family is unhappy in its own way* -

The sound of the train is blood red in my head.

The Slighted Piper

I sit alone by the fire and observe. My head tilted in a certain fashion so that they can't see me watching.

Clustered and laughing around the bar are the musicians with their instrument cases. The larger ones leaning against their owners' legs, the smaller cases still slung over coated backs.

In the far corner near the door sit an elderly couple, the man observing the world through gold-rimmed glasses perched on the end of his nose. He sits upright, and grasped in his gnarled and twisted hands are two wooden walking sticks. The sticks and his hands share the same hue, the same polish. His wife, sits further into the corner, she has small black eyes and grey wisped hair. She leans forward in her seat clutching a penny whistle to her chest, alert as a bird.

I wish the musicians would come and sit down, start to play. I keep glancing at the clock. An hour has passed, and now another half hour. Yet again they have refilled their glasses. My pint glass is half empty. It will have to last me all evening. I've lost the courage to go alone to the bar. From the basket beside the chimney I take a log and place it on the fire.

At ten thirty, a tall man with straw stubble hair comes and sits down. He removes his coat and unzips a fiddle from a soft brown case. He places it with its bow on the table. He doesn't acknowledge our presence, and I am glad that he does not recognise me. The other musicians follow his lead, swarming around the tables, undoing their cases; guitarists elbowing to ensure they have enough space to move their hands up and down the frets.

I shuffle further along my seat, nearer to the fire. The elderly woman looks anxiously around. When everyone is finally seated she picks up her empty glass and squeezes between the tables. I watch as she goes to the bar and orders a pint of Guinness and a half of sweet cider. As she returns, carrying the drinks, the fiddler begins to play. I can see in her eyes that it is a tune she knows. She inclines her head, smiles to herself, waiting at the edge of the room for the song to finish. The other musicians listen intently. A few join in, ears alert for a chord sequence they can follow. When the fiddle player finishes he looks around the room and picks another musician to play. I notice that sometimes he goes clockwise around the room and sometimes he picks at random, keeping them on their toes.

I watch the elderly woman as she sits, attentive, waiting her turn, her penny whistle placed in front of her on the table, but she is never invited to play. All evening the music goes round and round, more people arrive and are asked to play; glasses are refilled at the bar, the fiddler's pints brought to his table by the landlord.

I glance again at the clock. It is half past twelve. The elderly woman has still not been asked. I watch as she picks up her whistle from the table and lets her fingers dance silently up and down the length.

The room waits while the fiddle player chalks his bow. He starts low and soft, playing only to soothe himself. I pull my coat around my shoulders, stare into the dying fire.

Without warning, the elderly man pushes forward his table, scraping it noisily across the floor. The fiddler opens his eyes and scowls. I watch as the old man, ignoring him, leans heavily upon the table and stumbles to standing. His wife passes him his sticks and hurriedly puts on her coat.

I take my chance and follow them out into the night. It has started to snow and the first flakes catch in my hair. I hear a strange sound moving rapidly up the hill, like a child pulling an empty sledge on tarmac. The old man is skimming up the street with his sticks; the leather soles of his shoes glancing the road. His wife is hurrying along beside him. I watch as the derelict church catches the first snowflakes.

On the brow of the hill the wife stops. She turns and in her hands she grasps her penny whistle. She plays into the empty night: *The Fields of Athenry.*

> *By a lonely prison wall*
> *I heard a young girl calling ...*

Behind me, the music in the pub is stilled.

I clasp my hand around the warmth of the harmonica in my pocket, and walk away into the growing storm.

Nothing Stays the Same

You have checked in your luggage, gone through security and now you have an hour to wait until your flight to Istanbul. Your nephew had not realised that once through customs there would be nowhere to smoke, and nor had you, or you would have delayed your check-in, taken pity on him.

He seeks an outside place, even one drag would do, but there is nowhere. He tells you he will have to endure the next hour and the four and a half hour flight and then the wait at the other end, all without a cigarette. He's not sure how he's going to manage.

The year is 2010, the month is June, the date the third. You don't have to fly out of Heathrow for Istanbul these days. You are flying out of Exeter of all places; it is the nearest airport to your nephew's barracks. He has three days off to accompany you.

You are returning after thirty years, after you said you never would. You have agreed to attend the wedding of the son of an English friend, a friend who had stayed, even when her marriage had failed, enabled her children to become Turkish.

The wedding is to be a lavish affair, many dignitaries will be attending even, it is rumoured, some high up politicians.

108

You have chosen a simple dress for the wedding. It is not that you don't care about your appearance, just that you know that you will have to fade into the background, to be unknown. You had chosen carefully, remembered all the rules of how a good Muslim woman should dress, but the light in the shop must have been poor because when you'd tried the dress on at home you'd seen to your horror that it was partially transparent – the lining coming to only to just below your bottom. You'd solved the problem by bringing your long silk nightdress to wear as a petticoat.

You do not fly into Atatürk Havalimani as you always had done, driving in along by the Marmara shoreline, seeing Istanbul gradually appear, the minarets spiking the skyline.

Istanbul now has more than one airport, this one has grand marble halls and you smile when you find that you now have to pay to get into this country. You remember all those years ago when your then husband had asked you to smuggle American dollars out in a samovar, and how you had very nearly got caught, but at the last minute how they'd waved you through knowing you were English, as your husband said they would.

You do not speak to the taxi driver but show him the address of your friend.

Your nephew sits in the front, asks you if he can smoke. You ask can he wait, and he says no.

You try to remember your Turkish but the only relevant word you can bring to mind is, 'cigarette?' The taxi driver shakes his head; you remember the confusion in the past; how a shake of the head meant, 'yes'.

You could tell your nephew, he says no, but you don't.

'You can smoke,' you tell him.

He passes you a new packet to open for him. It is a task he finds difficult since losing the lower part of his left arm. You unwrap the cellophane wrapper, cup the lid open with your thumb, remove the foil wrapper, and lift one cigarette up an inch. You pass him the packet and, he is just about to put it to his mouth, when the driver leans over and takes one. The one you had lifted for your nephew. He laughs, surprised. You say, the taxi driver thought you'd asked if he wanted one.

The driver thanks your nephew, 'teşekkür.' He pulls the lighter out from the dashboard and offers it to your nephew before lighting his own, and you smile to yourself. How easy it is for men to reach that level of intimacy, of camaraderie, even when they don't speak the same language. And there you are, out there on the fringes as always.

You are on a motorway. You could be in any city; you see nothing that you recognise, miles and miles of square buildings of concrete and glass. Where is your Istanbul of sea and minarets and narrow streets?

You arrive at a gated community, a block of flats, and your friend comes down to greet you, she speaks to the taxi driver in fluent Turkish.

There are other English guests, you had not known this, two ladies who have taxied in from Atatürk

Havalimani. They tell you it has taken them three hours. They take your nephew under their wing and he smiles a half-smile, asks your friend if he can smoke out on her balcony.

Your friend tells you that her daughter has ordered pizza and beer online, and you are amazed at how modern Turkey has become. You say you've never heard of people in England ordering takeaways online and your nephew tells you he does it all the time

The next morning your friend's daughter drives you out of Istanbul, on a motorway that wasn't built when you were last here. Your nephew sits in the front with her, asks if he can smoke, '*Yok*,' she tuts, 'No you can't.' When did Turkish women become so assertive? you wonder.

The wedding is to be held in the home town of your friend's ex-husband: the town where he is known, where he holds power.

The journey is a blank, nothing makes any impression, except when you stop in a small town to get cash from a bank machine, you see a horse and cart parked next to a large grey Mercedes; after all these years, the old and new still sit side by side.

The hotel is on the side of a lake. Your friend and the other English guests arrive in a people carrier, sent especially for them. The dresses of your friend and her daughter are carried from the car in special bags draped over the arm of the driver.

You are shown to your room; it is more sophisticated than you had imagined and you realise this is the first time you have ever stayed in a hotel in this country. You have a view out over the lake as you requested.

Later in the afternoon, you go for a walk with your nephew. People stare openly at his limp sleeve. You hear him muttering obscenities under his breath, 'Wait till I get my metal hand, I'll show the bastards.'

You wander through the vendors down by the lake seeking foods you loved back then. You buy cherries as round and polished as conkers, the man makes a cocked hat out of newspaper and tips them in and presents them to you, but when he sees you go to eat one he shouts and takes them from you pouring them into a bowl, to wash under a tap before returning them to you in a fresh cocked hat. You remember then about unwashed fruit and how one always had to peel a peach. He smiles at you, nodding his head. You see he has a broken tooth. You remember that you must not smile back, must not show your weakness.

You bow your head, tell him '*Teşekkür ederim,*' thank you very much

Your nephew says he has had enough of these people gawping at him so you wander back to the hotel. On your way you see the garden of the wedding hotel with the tables already set out for the evening: a sea of white cloths, even the chairs with their own white covers.

The hotel where you are staying is quiet, the quiet of a mid-to-late afternoon in a hot country. Your friend and her daughter have gone to get their hair done.

Nothing Stays the Same

You do not feel like sleep; you are too ill at ease, you wish you were on a plane on your way home; there is something about this place that unnerves you still. The charade of it all, the way the waiters look at you with that imperceptible air of distaste, their discomfort in never quite knowing how to pigeon hole you other than a western woman. If you'd arrived dripping in gold, showing obvious wealth, then maybe they would have known how to serve you; they could understand wealth. It comes back to you: the Turkish for very rich, *çok zengin*. It had intrigued you, this phrase you kept hearing, over and over again, usually followed by an aah of admiration. You'd asked your then husband what does this mean, *çok zengin*?

You sit with your nephew at a table in the hotel garden near the lake. Tell him if he wants a drink he'd better catch the waiter's eye; they might take notice of him.

You had imagined the Black Sea coast to be beautiful. Your husband had told you all those years ago of the hazelnut groves that his family owned. He'd painted pictures of hills lined with tea plantations, of the high plateaux dense with hazelnut groves, and of clapboard houses, and all you have seen is blank countryside and more concrete squares, whole villages of them. The lake that you had expected to be thronged with boats is silent, the water dull, a mat of weed just below the surface. Maybe it is you, maybe you cannot see the beauty here, maybe you don't want to.

You smile, remembering the hazelnuts delivered in white cotton sacks, the tops sewn closed in brightly coloured threads, and when you'd unpicked the hand sewn threads, there inside were the wooden shells, their pale green caps still fresh from the mountain.

You are joined by the two English women and then your friend and her daughter. They discuss whether they should have a little something to eat, and what will be served at the wedding feast and when. Your friend knows only that no alcohol will be served. You order beer, white wine and a bowl of chips to share, wait for the clock to tick round. Your nephew orders himself more beer.

At six you go to dress, arrange that you will go slightly later than your friend and her daughter, and that you will meet the other women back in the foyer at six thirty.

You feel the sun on your back; it still has some heat as if it is only late afternoon and not early evening. The lakeshore is now thronged with vendors and people enjoying the evening. They stare at your party, at your wedding finery, in that unabashed way you remember now from all those years ago.

You listen to your new friends from England. You are glad that they are with you. The older of the two ladies is dressed in a beautiful peacock blue dress, her blonde hair, coiffed and styled to complement her outfit. She is going to show the Turks how the English can scrub up. You feel drab in comparison and wonder if you should you have made more of an effort, but it is too late now. You had thought your killer heels would add an element of style, make you walk tall, but your feet have swollen in the heat and, like one of the ugly sisters, you have not been able to squash your feet into your shoes. You have had to wear your flip-flops; you are glad your dress is long. Your nephew looks very handsome in his black suit and you tell him his mother would be very proud, but he only grunts.

He wants to buy some rakı; he can't believe it, a wedding without alcohol, had she known this beforehand? He doesn't know that you've known for months, that you've purposely not told him.

He's going to get some rakı and put it in a water bottle, he's decided. He intends to get drunk. You tell him, no, he mustn't, he must think of your friend; what an awkward position she would be in if anyone were to find out.

He takes no notice and enters a roadside kiosk.

Just as he does so a police car pulls up and two policemen get out, it is then that you see your friend in the peacock blue dress, waver - at first you think it is a trick of the light - but no, she is swaying, veering out into the road, into the traffic. You run, catch her arm to keep her upright but you are not strong enough. One of the policemen comes to your aid, he probably thinks she is drunk. Together you steady her, guide her to a white plastic chair that an old village woman outside the kiosk has kindly vacated. You sit her down, put her head between her knees, pray she is not seriously ill, not in this country, please god.

The old woman fetches a bottle of water, you thank her for her kindness, ask her how much you owe her. She clucks her tongue; removes the pale blue plastic top off the water bottle. You think she is offering your friend a drink; it is only at the last minute you realise that she is going to pour the water over her head.

You grab the old woman's wrist just in time. '*Yok*,' you say, '*yok*.'

But she is insistent, '*Evet, evet*.' Yes, yes.

It takes all your strength to stay her arm.

Annoyed she huffs off behind the kiosk, without even offering your friend a drink of the water.

Your nephew comes out of the kiosk. You snatch the bottle of water he has tucked under his arm. You cannot get the top off and go to hand it back for him to remove the top for you before remembering. You give it a final wrench and it comes off. Out of the corner of your eye you see him slip a glass bottle of rakı into his jacket pocket where it fits perfectly.

'Where were you?' you say. You explain what has happened. 'Why do you always disappear when you are most needed? And you're not taking that raki in,' you tell him. 'Not in that bottle anyway.'

This time he complies and you wonder if it is out of guilt. He pours the remainder of the water out onto the grass and then placing the bottle on the table pours in the rakı. You watch as he struggles, but you do not offer to help.

Your friend is regaining her colour. You don't tell her that she nearly had her wedding outfit spoiled. You

116

and her friend steady her, and you ask if she would prefer to go back to the hotel. She assures you that she will be fine and you admire her courage. She says it must have been the white wine on an empty stomach.

You walk with her slowly down through the chestnut avenue to the gate of the wedding hotel.

Your friend is there to greet the guests. She is wearing a long black dress with long sleeves. She stands opposite her ex-husband and his new wife who greet you with a stiff politeness.

You see the look of relief on her face when she sees you. Her friends are to be the kâfirs, the infidels, the people that are only here because the ex-wife cannot be excluded, not totally. For the first time you are glad you have come, that you are there to support your friend.

Your friend's daughter takes you to your table. You are bowled over by her dress; not since you were a fashion student back in the seventies and visited the Paris salons have you seen anything so exquisite. You tell her so and she smiles shyly, says her mum wouldn't let her wear jeans.

You are seated at a round table, to the left of the gate, the groom's side. The kind ex-brother-in-law and his family are to sit with you, to make up the numbers. The waiters hover, topping up the water, pouring it as if it were champagne.

You watch the other guests arrive, some like your friend's daughter are in sumptuous gowns, others are in beige raincoats with scarves tied under their chins, like factory workers from the fifties. You remember the countless attempts to make you wear a headscarf. It was the one thing you had held out against: you hated anything that covered your head, your ears, anything that closed you down. Still do.

Some of the later guests arrive in check shirts and jeans, both the men and the women. Your friend's daughter explains that the more distant a relative you are, the less important you are to the family, and the more casually you must dress.

There seems to be no sense of occasion regarding the food. You wait for everyone to start but this does not happen. Everyone eats at will in bits and bats and when they have finished a course the waiter takes away their plate and brings the next dish.

You look across at your nephew; he has his sullen face on. You'd thought it such a good idea when your sister first suggested he accompany you here, but now you're not so sure. You can't gauge him these days, not since the accident; he seems to have gone into himself.

The bride and groom arrive. The bride looks like a Hollywood film actress but not for long you think, once she has dropped a few babies, once she is crushed, though maybe that doesn't happen now. You wonder.

Your friend has to stand at the front for the wedding ceremony with her son and his bride and her ex-husband. You are too far away to hear what is happening. When it is over your friend comes back to sit down, glad it is over. The bride and groom begin to circulate the tables, thanking everyone for coming. Behind them walk your friend's daughter and another girl holding large velvet bags into which we all drop our gift of gold. You remember the tale of your ex-sister-in-law's wedding and how she had three armfuls of gold bangles.

Next comes the cake, taller than the bride and groom, who carry it between them. It looks strange, light somehow, and your friend tells you it is made of cardboard and later, when you go to the toilet, you see it lying lopsided in the hallway.

The young women in their designer dresses dance, gyrating like belly dancers with their men. The headscarves look on disapprovingly and you can almost hear the cluck of their tongues behind their front teeth. Your friend leans over and tells you that anyone who had any sense got drunk before they arrived. You see your nephew empty his glass of water, undo the top of the water bottle with his teeth, pour in the rakı, down it in one, then pour in some more. A waiter circles and quick as a flash you see him pour water into your nephew's glass, see the liquid as it turns to a thin milky liquid, swirling accusingly as it takes hold. The waiter sees it and shouts across to the headwaiter, but a politician has arrived and he has more important things to attend to.

You shout at your nephew, 'For god's sake drink it down.'

'Oh my god,' your friend puts her hand to her mouth. 'Oh god, if he's caught I'll be in such shit.'

You go round to your nephew, snatch the water bottle out of his pocket, go to the toilet, again past the lopsided wedding cake, and pour the raki down the toilet.

You sit the wedding out for another hour and then make your escape, with your new English friends, promising your nephew that he can have a drink back at the hotel. But as you enter your hotel you see the waiters are just leaving.

You ask if you can get a drink. They look you up and down, '*Yok*,' they say, '*yok*.'

You tell your nephew, Never mind there will be a mini bar in the room, knowing full well there won't be.

He asks why you dragged him here to this country. You don't remind him that he offered to come; that he wanted to see the place that you'd told him stories of when he was a child.

You let him go upstairs and then go to stand by the side of the lake. It is pitch black. There is a cacophony rising from the water, a cacophony of frogs that you cannot see: a deep bass with an undertone of gravel. There must be hundreds of them; you will ask your friend in the morning what kind they are. All through the night their chorus resonates until you see the space under the hem of the curtain begin to lighten, then they fall silent.

The next day you travel back to Istanbul. Your friend has promised to take you down to the waterfront, to the Istanbul you remember.

You take two taxis down to the shore. Your friend has gone in the other taxi, knowing that at least you can speak some Turkish. The journey seems to take forever, and you are not sure whether this is because of the traffic, or the distance, or both. You have never travelled in this part of the city before, never knew it existed. You cannot get your bearings and pray your friend is there, waiting for you when you arrive. Suddenly, you are there by the water and you let out a sigh of relief. But nothing looks the same. It is busier, dirtier, noisier than you remember. You can't find the heart of the place, the place you loved. It seems now to be a city much like any other. Where are the porters who wore their harnesses of leather to carry furniture through the narrow streets? Where are the street vendors, the young boys trying to sell bottled water straight from the tap, or the illegal cigarette sellers, running through the streets shouting the names of foreign cigarettes? The vendors are now men, seedy men who pester you in an unwholesome way and your friend tells them in Turkish to stop, but they follow her along the street, mocking her accent. You do not remember this disrespect from before.

Your friend says that we will get a ferry across the Bosphorus, and your heart lifts. Of all the things you remember, it is the ferries that bring back the fondest memories: leaving behind the turmoil of Istanbul, sailing out into the Marmara to the little islands devoid of traffic, just forty minutes from the city. The forests of pines with widespread branches, the Greek monastery high on the hill above the trees.

Your friend says the Islands have not changed, are still the same, she goes to the biggest island, the one furthest away, to cycle the path through the pine trees, to listen to the wind from the sea as it sifts the branches.

Nothing Stays the Same

You remember: the tea sellers on the ferries, whirling the decks like dervishes with huge round trays of clinking tea glasses held aloft with one hand, '*çay, çay, çay.*' The ayran sellers: yoghurt and mint, glasses with no saucers or spoons for the sugars, the man selling fresh split walnuts, so fresh that the white sap still seeped from them.

As you board the boat you point out the *No Smoking* sign to your nephew. He grunts, goes off down the other side of the boat; you hope he isn't going to chance it. The boat is silent, there is no rat-a-tat-tat of the tea or ayran sellers, just a silent man with a basket selling packs of highly-coloured sweets. The ferries are the same ferries you remember: the same maroon leather benches, but oh, it all looks so tired. Had it been so back then? Had you seen it through different eyes? Why did nothing ever get better? Why did nothing stay the same?

As the ferry makes its way across the water, you look back at the skyline of the city, each building rising higher than the one below; all the way up the hillside to the horizon.

'Each vying for a view,' your friend says.

The minarets are still there, more of them, but they no longer hold the skyline. You ask about the population, and your friend says it has doubled since you were last there.

You disembark at the ferry terminus across the water and search anxiously for your nephew. He is there, silent: tucking in behind you so no one will see his arm. You relax a little and realise that this is the ferry terminus that you always came to, to catch the ferry to and from the islands. You glance into the waiting room with its leather benches and remember sitting there with your then husband. Him telling you to lower your eyes or he would get into a fight; ranting at you later, back at the flat - was I a prostitute, was I so stupid as to smile at a man? How dare I spoil his honour! You were bewildered. It was your natural bent, when smiled at, to smile back. It had never occurred to you not to do so. You knew what flirting was, but you were not flirting. You had learnt to undo those ways.

We cross the road to the main Istanbul station, the destination of the Orient Express, where Europe stops and Asia begins. You had always wanted to travel from this station but never had.

You wait for the bus to take you to the Topkapi district, to visit the underground waterways, the Basilica Cistern.

It is tranquil below the city. You do not remember having been here before, not until a year later when leafing through your mother's photo album. You came here with your mother and stepfather. That one time when you were freer, visited more places, when everyone clustered around your step-father calling him 'Profesör', a title he rarely used, and how your mother dealt with the strangeness of it all by having her inevitable migraine. On one occasion you had cajoled her into going out to tea with you and your mother-in-law to visit the home of a relative. She had looked at you, puzzled, that you could be so easy among these strange women.

123

This is the area of the city that you remember, the houses are older, the streets narrower, but it has lost its uniqueness - it is now just a tourist trap, a place to wander aimlessly.

There are no soldiers on street corners as there were once when you came, after a military coup, when the prime minister had been executed. You remember telling your then husband how afraid the soldiers made you feel, and he had laughed and said they made him feel safer, he liked it better when there was a coup, things were always more stable. You must tell your nephew this story.

You go into a posh hotel on the waterfront and take a lift to the rooftop bar, drink a beer and smile to yourself. You would never have been brought here thirty years ago. You point out the islands to your nephew, green mounds dotted on the horizon; you tell him how beautiful they are and he asks how you get to them. You watch the sun set and concede that it is still as glorious as it ever was.

You get the bill and your friend works out that we have been overcharged. You do not leave a tip.

You make your way back down towards the railway station. You take the arm of the peacock lady, who now no longer wears her peacock dress, you tell her you are going to make sure she doesn't veer out into the traffic again and you both laugh with relief.

You are going to get taxis back across town, across the bridge where your friend has to collect tickets for an Amy Winehouse concert.

Nothing Stays the Same

A pop concert in Istanbul, you smile to yourself, were there such things back then? Were you not told of them? Were they what the non-believers attended?

Again you are in two taxis. Your nephew does not ask if he can smoke this time but takes out his pack and does not offer the taxi driver one. You are frightened. It is dark now, you keep looking behind, to see if your friend is following. Your taxi is hurtling through the traffic, weaving from lane to lane. Will you die in this city? You could close your eyes but then you won't be able to check if your friend is still behind you. You turn around; she is not there. The driver is asking you questions and you can't think of the words. Where are they? Why don't they come? He pulls over and you are glad to see a big poster of Amy Winehouse's face outside a theatre.

You get out of the taxi, go around to the back of the car, you want to face the taxi driver when you ask him how much. You had forgotten your friend's advice, forgotten to ask how much before you got in. The driver gets out, comes round to meet you, as you step off the pavement, you tread on a flattened plastic water bottle, it slides your foot out from under you. You feel yourself moving out into the stream of traffic, falling. The driver does not come to your aid but your nephew does. He is there trying to lift you, drag you away from the traffic and just that one word.

'Auntie.' You hear the concern in his voice. You want to cry, to be away from the bewilderment of this place. You wish you'd never come back and you are ashamed of your weakness. You have travelled the world and never been afraid like this before.

Your friend's taxi draws up just as you have regained your composure. Like the incident before the wedding with the peacock lady, the telling would in no way explain the awfulness of it so you do not try.

You go to a garden restaurant down by the seashore, but you cannot see the water because it is dark now and there are tall buildings in the way. You cannot see what you are eating and are cautious about what you order, remembering tales of aunts that would ask to inspect the kitchens before sitting down for a meal. You wonder if this still happens. You feel so odd here, eating in a posh restaurant; you feel like a child doing something wrong, something not allowed. You know how these waiters view you, even now thirty years older, only you and your friend know they see you as little more than prostitutes. The two other English women think we are being treated with respect but you see the little signs, the offhandedness, the way our plates are slapped on the table. Your nephew is too busy trying to eat one-handed to notice anything, and you are glad.

The next morning you are up early, too early and, unexpectedly, so is your nephew. Your friend says it will take an hour, tops, to get to the airport even in the rush hour traffic, but you are taking no chances. You make her order the taxi three hours before you are due at the airport and when you get on the motorway you are glad you have done so for the traffic is standing and there is miles and miles of it. What if you were to get stuck here in this country? You just want to be gone, to look down from the plane, see Istanbul and the gentle green rise of the islands far below.

You try to remember your Turkish to say that you must be at the airport at a certain time. You see the driver's puzzled face in his rear view mirror and, whether it is desperation or the few days you have spent here, suddenly your language is there in your mouth, after all those years.

'*Anliyor mi,*' - do you understand?' you say, after you have told him the time of the plane.

'*Anliyorum.*' I understand, he says.

He starts to edge his way into the inside lane and then onto the hard shoulder. You don't know if this is legal or not but you don't care. All you want him to do is to speed faster and faster along the hard shoulder, closer and closer to the airport. You look in your purse; see that you have double the Turkish Lira you need for the fare. You swear if he gets you there on time he can have it all. You don't want it; you are never coming back.

He drives erratically speeding up and slowing down and then jamming on his brakes, coming to a complete halt behind stationary white vans that stop without warning to pick up itinerant workers at the side of the motorway. And you want to laugh at the anarchy of the place and how it makes you suddenly feel.

You never found that here, in this country, never found the freedom, maybe it only belonged to the men.

About the Author

Bryony Doran won the first ever Hookline Novel Competition with her novel, The China Bird. She is currently working on her second novel and a collection of poetry.

www.bryonydoran.com

Also by Bryony Doran
The China Bird

A young art student sees beauty in Edward's twisted spine and begs him to sit for her. Wary but flattered, Edward sheds his clothing and emerges from years of concealment.

Book groups said:
'A beautifully written book, excellent description of human emotion, how life changes after certain events.'

Read an excerpt:
http://www.hooklinebooks.com/the-china-bird.php

Lightning Source UK Ltd.
Milton Keynes UK
UKOW04f0249201113

221467UK00003B/8/P